THE SLEEPING PRINCESS

Barbara Cartland

Barbara Cartland Ebooks Ltd

This edition © 2018

ISBNs

9781788671514   EPUB

9781788671521   PAPERBACK

Book design by M-Y Books
m-ybooks.co.uk

THE BARBARA CARTLAND ETERNAL COLLECTION

The Barbara Cartland Eternal Collection is the unique opportunity to collect all five hundred of the timeless beautiful romantic novels written by the world's most celebrated and enduring romantic author.

Named the Eternal Collection because Barbara's inspiring stories of pure love, just the same as love itself, the books will be published on the internet at the rate of four titles per month until all five hundred are available.

The Eternal Collection, classic pure romance available worldwide for all time .

THE LATE DAME BARBARA CARTLAND

Barbara Cartland, who sadly died in May 2000 at the grand age of ninety eight, remains one of the world's most famous romantic novelists. With worldwide sales of over one billion, her outstanding 723 books have been translated into thirty six different languages, to be enjoyed by readers of romance globally.

Writing her first book 'Jigsaw' at the age of 21, Barbara became an immediate bestseller. Building upon this initial success, she wrote continuously throughout her life, producing bestsellers for an astonishing 76 years. In addition to Barbara Cartland's legion of fans in the UK and across Europe, her books have always been immensely popular in the USA. In 1976 she achieved the unprecedented feat of having books at numbers 1 & 2 in the prestigious B. Dalton Bookseller bestsellers list.

Although she is often referred to as the 'Queen of Romance', Barbara Cartland also wrote several historical biographies, six autobiographies and numerous theatrical plays as well as books on life, love, health and cookery. Becoming one of Britain's most popular media personalities and dressed in her trademark pink, Barbara spoke on radio and television about social and political issues, as well as making many public appearances.

In 1991 she became a Dame of the Order of the British Empire for her contribution to literature and her work for humanitarian and charitable causes.

Known for her glamour, style, and vitality Barbara Cartland became a legend in her own lifetime. Best remembered for her wonderful romantic novels and loved by millions of readers worldwide, her books remain treasured for their heroic heroes, plucky heroines and traditional values. But above all, it was Barbara Cartland's overriding belief in the positive power of love to help, heal and improve the quality of life for everyone that made her truly unique.

AUTHOR'S NOTE

It was at the beginning of the seventeenth century that the English aristocrats became connoisseurs and began making collections for their Stately Homes.

The greatest portrait painter of the era was Sir Anthony Van Dyck and it is thought that he was seen first in Rubens's Studio in Antwerp by travelling Noblemen.

It was men like Thomas Howard the Earl of Arundel, who persuaded Van.Dyck to come to England.

After eleven years, when his skill was known and admired all over Europe, he returned to England for a second time to begin a series of portraits of the Royal Family.

His triple portrait of King Charles I was a brilliant example of his skill.

Another of Van Dyck's wonderful portraits was of Thomas Wentworth the Earl of Stafford, while others were of Lord Derby and the Earl of Penbrook.

It became a trademark of every Van Dyck picture that the hands of his subject, with their thin aristocratic fingers, were outstanding and different from the hands painted by any other artist.

CHAPTER ONE
1874

As the carriage turned into Grosvenor Square, Lady Odela Ford was feeling nervous.

All the way from Florence she had been thinking excitedly about coming home and seeing her father again.

Now, although she tried not to, she felt apprehensive.

After a year of misery and loneliness when her mother had died, her father, the Earl of Shalford, had married again rather too rapidly.

He had told her in a somewhat embarrassed manner that he intended to marry a widow, Lady Dean.

Odela could remember her dismay at this news all too vividly.

She had already met Lady Dean and she thought somewhat scornfully that she was fawning on her father in an exaggerated way.

Odela loved him and understood how desperately he missed her mother as she did. .She was therefore too tactful to make any protest.

Esme Dean had then taken over the house, even before the Wedding took place very quietly.

Odela had to admit that her stepmother was very attractive and she always said the most flattering things to everybody she met.

Everything she did, anywhere she went, was 'too wonderful for words' and she never spoke to her husband without complimenting him on his brains, his looks and his exalted position in life.

At first Odela chided herself for being critical and then she knew instinctively that this was an exaggerated pose that was invariably hypocritical.

It had nothing to do with her stepmother's real feelings.

In a way Odela was not surprised when, immediately after the Wedding was over, the new Countess began to say to her husband,

"Odela is so clever, darling, just like you, and we must be careful that we don't waste her brain."

To Odela herself she would say,

"It's quite unnecessary for you to be both pretty and clever. You should not work so hard and spoil your beautiful eyes."

Odela soon found that these remarks were merely stepping stones.

Her stepmother had decided that she should go abroad to what was known as a 'Finishing School'.

There were in fact two or three in England, but the Countess considered that they were not good enough.

"I am told by the most reliable people," she said to the Earl, "that the Seminary for Young Ladies in Florence is noted for its brilliant teachers."

She paused before she added with a smile,

"The aristocrats from every country in Europe send their daughters there and what could be better for dear little Odela than to be able to speak French and Italian fluently?"

Odela had not objected because she knew that it was hopeless to do so.

She was also finding it hard to tolerate the many changes her stepmother was making in their two houses that had been her mother's pride and joy.

Fortunately, Odela thought, the new Countess was not particularly interested in Shalford Hall in the country.

In London the old servants were dismissed and new faces were brought in to take their place.

Odela, as it happened was extremely intelligent.

She knew that it would be foolish and unkind to her father if, as soon as he had remarried, she quarrelled with her stepmother.

He was quite obviously besotted with his young and beautiful wife. He would therefore not have been prepared to listen to anything that was said against her.

Then the moment came when the Countess said in direct tones,

"I have news for you, dearest Odela, which I am sure will please you. You know, dear child, that all I want is your happiness, but I also want you to be a huge success when you become a *debutante*."

She paused and, as Odela did not speak, she then went on,

"Your father, who in his marvellous way is always thinking of other people rather than himself, has agreed that you should go to Florence for a year!"

She gave a little laugh, which her admirers always said was like the tinkling of bells, before she continued,

"I know that there you will learn to be as clever as your wonderful father and also have all the graces that every woman should have if she is to shine in London Society."

Odela drew in her breath, but had merely asked,

"When do you want me to leave, Papa?"

"Immediately!" her stepmother answered for him, "and you will return at exactly the same time next year when I know you will burst like a meteor on London and dazzle us all."

She gave another laugh before she added,

"You are a lucky, lucky girl! And, of course, it is all due to your kind and understanding father, who I know will miss you while you are away."

Odela had forced herself to say that she was grateful for the opportunity.

At the same time she was well aware that her stepmother had got her own way and achieved what she had set out to do.

She had, however, experienced a shock when she went upstairs.

She learnt that her Nanny, who had been with her ever since she was born, had been told that her services were no longer required.

It was then she had flung her arms around her neck exclaiming,

"You cannot leave, Nanny, I cannot lose you! Mama always said you would stay with us all your life!"

"Your mother, God rest her soul, said the same thing to me," Nanny replied, "but her Ladyship has other ideas."

"I will speak to Papa! I cannot let you go!" Odela cried.

"It won't be any use, dearie," Nanny answered. "Her Ladyship'll get her way and she wants all the old staff out so that she can bring in those who toady to her!"

"But how can I manage without you?" Odela asked helplessly, the tears running down her cheeks.

"You're goin' away for a year," Nanny said, "and when you come back perhaps her Ladyship'll let me return to maid you."

"Oh, Nanny, do you think she will?" Odela enquired.

Even as she spoke she knew that it was very unlikely.

The Countess had a smart French lady's maid, who went tittle-tatting to her with everything that went on in the household.

Odela was quite certain that her stepmother had sensed that Nanny did not like her and once she was out of the house she would never be able to return.

She cried bitterly when she had to say 'goodbye' to Nanny.

She wrote to her every week while she was away and she could not have told her father the problems and difficulties that she inevitably encountered in a strange school in a foreign land.

She just knew that Nanny would understand.

It made her feel better to put everything down on paper and be sure that Nanny would read it with love.

*

She thought now that everything would be very different if Nanny was waiting for her in Grosvenor Square.

As the carriage drew up outside Shalford House, she saw two strange footmen putting down the red carpet.

And there was an unfamiliar butler waiting for her in the doorway.

"Welcome home, my Lady," he said respectfully as she entered. "Her Ladyship's in her sitting room."

"Sitting room?" Odela queried.

"On the first floor, my Lady, next to her Ladyship's bedroom."

Odela remembered then that it had always been called a 'boudoir'.

Immediately after she was married the Countess had said,

"As I wish to entertain my friends in my own room, I think 'boudoir' sounds too intimate. In future I will call it my 'sitting room'."

"You can call it anything you like, my darling," the Earl replied, "as long as you are in it."

His wife's eyes looked up at him adoringly.

"Oh, Arthur, that is what I want you to think," she simpered, "and you know that, when I am working in my sitting room, it will be so that everything in the house is perfect for you."

Odela went up the stairs, conscious as she did so that the nervousness she had felt in the carriage had now intensified.

She told herself it was ridiculous and that there was nothing to fear or be frightened about.

While her brain said one thing, however, her instinct told her something different.

The butler opened the door and she saw at once that the room was completely changed from when her mother had used it.

The curtains, the covers and the carpet were all new and the antique furniture, which had been very attractive, had all been replaced with what was more ornate and flamboyant and much more modern.

There were marble-topped tables, which were carved and gilded and there was a far larger chandelier than in her mother's time.

The pictures had nearly all gone and instead there were gold-framed mirrors.

And they reflected the beauty of its new occupant.

As Odela appeared, the Countess rose from the chair where she had been sitting and held out both her hands.

"Odela!" she exclaimed. "How delightful to see you."

She kissed her on both cheeks.

Then she put her hands on her shoulders to hold her away from her.

"How pretty you have grown," she remarked. "Yes, very very pretty! You will be the belle of every ball I will take you to!"

It all sounded very convincing.

Odela. However. sensed, although she told herself that it was unreasonable, that there was something behind all this.

Something that she could not put a name to, but which was undoubtedly there.

"Now sit down," the Countess was saying, "and I will tell you just how much we have to do – "

"I hope, Stepmama," Odela interrupted, "that I will be able to go down to the country. I have been looking forward to riding Dragonfly."

"Dragonfly?" the Countess repeated in a perplexed tone. "Oh, your horse."

"Papa told me that he was well," Odela said, "and it is so lovely at The Hall in the spring!"

"Yes, I know, dear," the Countess agreed, "but you will know that the Season has started and we are booked to attend two or three parties nearly every night for the next three months."

Odela prevented herself from giving an exclamation of horror.

And then the Countess went on,

"Of course, you will have to have some new clothes and your father in his usual generous open-handed way, has said that I can buy you anything I think necessary. What a wonderful, wonderful man he is!"

"I have some quite pretty clothes," Odela replied, "which I bought in Florence."

The Countess laughed a little scornfully.

"Florence! Most of the smart clothes in London come from Paris and when you see them you will realise that there is nothing like French *chic* and an elegance that is unattainable anywhere else in the world."

Odela did not argue, she merely listened.

She felt her heart sink at the idea that she should be confined in London for the Season.

She wanted to go to Shalford Hall, which was in the most beautiful part of Oxfordshire.

All the way home from Florence she had been thinking of the crocuses, white, purple and yellow, flowering under the oak trees.

The snowdrops and the violets in the greenery and the golden kingcups all round the lake.

"We shall have to work very fast," the Countess was saying. "There is a ball at Devonshire House next week and you must have something really spectacular for that occasion."

She smiled at Odela and then continued,

"I think too that your father intends to speak to the Prince of Wales so that you are included in one of the parties to be given at Marlborough House."

She paused before she added,

"Do you realise what a lucky, lucky girl you are to have such an important and distinguished father? *Debutantes* are never invited to Marlborough House."

Odela was thinking about Dragonfly.

She was planning in her mind how, even if she went to Shalford Hall for only one night, she must somehow see him.

She wanted to be quite sure that he was just as splendid as he had been before she went away.

She had owned Dragonfly since he was a foal and had trained him herself. He came when she called him and nuzzled against her to show his love.

He would take fences that the grooms thought were too high for her simply to show that he could do it.

The Countess was talking on about what colours would suit her and what gowns would be outstanding in any ballroom.

"Thank Goodness," she commented, "we have the bustle and not the crinoline. You will look absolutely lovely, Odela, with a bustle at the back of your gowns."

She smiled before she carried on,

"It's so exciting to think that money is no object."

She said the last sentence in such an ecstatic way that Odela looked at her in surprise.

"I am sure that Papa would not want me to be over-extravagant," she replied.

There was a little pause before the Countess said,

"Your father will tell you about that himself."

The way she spoke told Odela that there was something important that he had to tell her.

She wondered what it could possibly be.

*

That evening her father came back from the House of Lords obviously delighted to see her.

He held her close in his arms as he said,

"I have missed you, my dearest daughter!"

He looked at her searchingly and added, almost as if he was speaking to himself,

"You are so much like your mother. You are in fact almost identical to the way she looked when I married her."

There was a note in his voice that told Odela that he had not forgotten her mother.

"You could not have said anything, Papa," she replied, "that could please me more. If I was half as pretty as Mama, I would be very happy!"

"You are very pretty, my dear," her father said, "or perhaps the right word is 'lovely'."

They were in his study and Odela thought that he looked towards the door before he added,

"There will never be anybody like your mother and you must never forget her!"

"Of course I could never forget her," Odela responded. "I think of her every day and, when I pray to her, I feel that she is very near to me."

Her father put his hands on her shoulders.

"I am quite certain she is," he said quietly.

Then her stepmother came bustling into the study to say,

"Is it not delightful to have dear little Odela home with us? But now you must hurry and dress for dinner or you will both be late."

"I hope we don't have guests this evening?" the Earl asked rather pointedly.

The way he spoke told Odela that there were always guests at Grosvenor Square and at times he was bored with them.

The Countess slipped her arm through his.

"How can you imagine, dearest Arthur, that I would spoil the happiness of Odela's first evening back at home by having strangers with us."

She stopped speaking a moment before she continued.

"I want to hear what she has been learning and I know when dinner is over that you have something special to tell her."

The Earl frowned as if she had been indiscreet and the Countess walked towards the door as she was saying,

"Now, come along, Odela. You must make yourself look really lovely for your father and no one knows better than he does how important are the poise and polish you have obtained from a Cosmopolitan education."

They dined at a table that was large enough to accommodate at least thirty guests. It was decorated with golden candelabra and elaborate ornaments that her mother had only used on special occasions. There was also an arrangement of orchids on the table.

The flowers that decorated the drawing room where they met before dinner must, Odela thought, have cost a fortune.

She was wearing one of the pretty gowns that she had bought in Florence.

The dressmaker had told .her that it was the copy of a French model.

Odela saw her stepmother's eyes appraising her up and down and knew that despite herself she was impressed.

She said, however, in her usual gushing tone,

"Is it not lovely, Arthur, to have Odela with us? And I am so looking forward to presenting her to our friends and, of course, to Her Majesty Queen Victoria at her first 'drawing room'."

"I have arranged it, as you asked me to," the Earl pointed out somewhat heavily.

"I knew you would," the Countess replied. "You must thank your clever father, Odela, for as usual, he has been able to pull strings as no one else could do."

"Of course I am grateful, Papa," Odela said quickly, "but I am hoping that we shall have time to go home, before I am completely snowed under by engagements."

Her father looked at her and she knew by the expression in his eyes that he understood that by 'home' she meant their house in the country.

And not the London house where her mother had spent as little time as possible.

Before he could speak the Countess gave a cry.

"I have already told Odela, Arthur darling, that she will have to wait until the end of the Season before we return to The Hall."

The Earl did not speak and Odela said,

"I know you will understand, Papa, that I am longing to see Dragonfly. I loved reading about him in the letters you wrote to me. I must see him now that I am back from Florence."

"Yes, of course," the Earl said, "and, if we cannot manage anything longer, we will slip down to The Hall one Saturday night and stay through until Monday."

Even as Odela's eyes lit up, the Countess said,

"Of course, Arthur dearest, we will all go to the country if you want to, but some of the best balls I have already accepted for Odela take place on a Saturday night."

She paused and then put out her hand to lay it on his.

"But, dearest, it shall be exactly as you wish and we will manage it somehow, although it may be difficult."

Even as she spoke, Odela knew only too well that her stepmother would put every possible obstacle in the way of them going to the country even for a weekend.

But she was far too clever to say so.

From the way her father changed the subject she realised that he was as aware of this as she was.

They talked about other issues and the current political scene until dinner was over.

As they left the dining room, the Earl told the butler to bring a glass of brandy to his study.

"I know, dearest," the Countess said, "that you want to be alone with Odela. I have therefore asked two of my friends to join me after dinner."

The Earl looked surprised, but he merely replied,

"That is very tactful of you, my dear, I have a great deal to talk about to Odela."

"I always try to do what pleases you," the Countess said coyly and kissed him on the cheek.

Odela walked with her father along the passage to his study.

She was aware as she did so that her stepmother was running eagerly upstairs to the drawing room.

She thought that it was as if she was glad to be free of them. But it was just a passing thought.

Then, as Odela entered her father's study, she saw to her relief that it was the one room that was unchanged.

There were the same well-worn red leather sofa and armchairs.

The same large flat-topped desk piled with her father's papers.

And there were the same pictures of horses and dogs that she had loved so much as a child.

There were even more of them in her father's study in the country and she mused that he only felt at home when his sporting pictures were around him.

. "It is marvellous to see you again, Papa," she said. "I missed you so much when I was away for so long."

Impulsively she put her arms around his neck and kissed him.

"I would have liked you to come back for your holidays," her father told her, "but your stepmother felt that it might prevent you from concentrating on your studies."

Odela knew that her stepmother did not want her home, but she merely replied,

"Well, I have finished with that now, and I hope you will be pleased, Papa, at how much I have learnt."

"You are back home," he sighed, "and that is all that really matters."

He sat down on the red leather sofa and, when Odela sat beside him, he put his arm around her.

"I have so much to tell you," he said.

"What about?" Odela enquired.

She thought with surprise that he was feeling for words, but then he began,

"Do you remember your grandmother?"

"Do you mean Mama's mother?"

"Yes."

"Of course I remember her," Odela replied. "But she died when I was ten."

"Yes, I know," her father answered, "and she was particularly fond of you because you resembled your mother so closely."

"I remember her saying that," Odela said, "and she had that miniature of me painted which used to hang in Mama's boudoir."

As she spoke, she wondered what had happened to the miniature now.

Then her father said, as if she had asked him the question,

"I have it in the drawer of my desk and, when you compare it with that of your mother at about the same age, it is very difficult to tell you apart."

"It is wonderful to think that I am like Mama," Odela said with a little sigh.

She wanted to add that she was very thankful not to look like her stepmother.

Her mother had been very fair, but the new Countess had red lights in her brown hair, which Odela suspected were not entirely natural.

At the same time she was very pretty. But there was something superficial about her that there had never been in her mother's beauty.

"I always thought," her father said unexpectedly, "that your mother was the most beautiful woman I had ever seen in my life. But it was not only her beauty that made me love her."

Odela was listening intently as he went on,

"She had a spiritual quality about her that you, my darling, have as well. It is something that you cannot learn out of a book or be taught by somebody else, however wise."

He smiled at her as he carried on,

"It is something that comes from within you."

Odela put her head against his shoulder,

"Oh, Papa, I would rather you told me that than gave me the most marvellous wonderful present in the whole world!"

"I am speaking the truth," the Earl replied, "and it is something you will need in the future. You must promise me, Odela, that whatever you do and wherever you go, you will follow your instinct."

He spoke so seriously that Odela added,

"That is what I already try to do because Mama told me to use my instinct about people as she used hers."

"Your mother was right and it is advice you must never forget," her father declared.

"I will never forget anything that Mama said to me," Odela promised.

Then, as there was silence, she asked,

"Have you any reason for saying this to me, Papa?"

Her father smiled.

"Now you are using your instinct and the answer is a definite 'yes'!"

"What is it, Papa?" Odela enquired.

Somehow she suddenly felt frightened.

She realised that this must be the reason why she had felt nervous ever since she had arrived.

Her father now seemed to be feeling for words again.

Finally he said,

"Because your grandmother adored your mother, when she died she left her everything she possessed."

Odela was listening and the Earl continued,

"It was not very much at the time, just a few hundreds of pounds a year. Your mother when she died left everything to you. Now you are unexpectedly a very wealthy young woman!"

"I – I don't understand," Odela stammered. "I always imagined that Mama's family – was rather poor."

"That was true," the Earl said, "but before she died your grandmother was given some shares by her Godfather, who was an American."

"An American!" Odela exclaimed.

"I never remembered my brother-in-law or your mother speaking of him," her father went on, "but he came from Texas."

He paused a moment and then continued,

"Unfortunately, as we are rather insular, we were not particularly interested in anyone from across the Atlantic."

"But he left Grandmama – some money?" Odela said as if she was trying to understand the implications. "Why did Mama not – enjoy it?"

"That is what I have to explain to you," the Earl smiled.

But once again he seemed to be feeling for words before he went on,

"The shares that your mother received have in the last year increased enormously. They are in oil and oil in Texas means that those who possess shares are rapidly becoming millionaires!"

Odela stared at him.

"And you are saying, Papa, that this money is – now mine?"

"That is what I am telling you, my dearest, and it is, as you must realise, a very big responsibility."

"Oh, I wish that Mama had known!" Odela cried. "You know how much she longed to build schools in the villages on the estate and also a hospital."

"That is true," the Earl nodded, "but it was impossible to find sufficient funds for me to do so."

"Is this something I can do now?" Odela enquired.

"If you wish to, my dearest, but equally you must remember that you will not live for the rest of your life at The Hall."

Odela stared at him and he continued,

~21~

"You will, of course, be married and, while it will break my heart to lose you again, I want you to be as happy as I was with your mother."

Odela noticed that he did not say, 'as I am with Esme'.

"I pray, Papa," she answered, "that I will find a man I will love and who will love me as you loved Mama, but it is going to be difficult to find someone as marvellous as you."

"Now you are flattering me," her father laughed. "Of course you will find somebody, but at the same time you are going to find it difficult to avoid the fortune-hunters!"

"I have read about the fortune-hunters in books – and the girls at school used to laugh about the Italian aristocrats who were always on the lookout for a rich wife!"

"I am afraid there are a number of them in this country who do the same thing," the Earl said. "Therefore, my precious daughter, I have to do everything in my power to protect you from men who will find your money irresistible."

Odela sighed.

"I understand, Papa, exactly what you are saying to me and, of course, I shall be very careful."

She waited a moment and then went on,

"But I think if I use my instinct as Mama did I shall find a man like you and know at once that he loves me for myself."

"It's not easy," the Earl said. "I have seen all too often in my life young women being pursued the moment they appear as a *debutante* simply because it is known that a fortune goes with them."

"Then, as soon as I receive a proposal, if I do receive one," Odela suggested, "you shall use your instinct, Papa, and tell me if he is right or wrong."

The Earl gave a little laugh.

"It is not as easy as that. Some men have what your mother used to call 'honeyed tongues' and girls, however intelligent they are, can be swept off their feet. Quite frankly, my beautiful daughter, I am very worried."

"Oh, Papa, I don't want you to be worried about me!" Odela replied. "Let's go to the country and concentrate on the horses. Forget the young men who prefer glittering gold to a gallop on the flat land!"

The Earl laughed.

"I would love to do that," he said, "but you know as well as I do that I have my duties in the House of Lords and, of course, your stepmother has set her heart on introducing you to the Social world."

Odela's lips tightened for a moment.

Now she could understood why her stepmother had been making so much fuss of her since she had come home from Florence. There nothing she would enjoy more than the huge ball they could now afford to give.

Then there were the expensive gowns and the endless parties.

She would be invited to these not as a *debutante* but as a girl with a golden halo.

Impulsively she now said,

"I suppose, Papa, that there is no chance of my being able to – refuse this money?"

"Refuse it?" the Earl questioned her.

"I don't want it. You loved Mama not because of what she had or did not have but for herself. There must be a man somewhere – who will love me in the same way."

"There will be a great number of men who will love you for yourself," her father replied. "At the same time there will be a larger number who will be attracted to you because, as you well know, the moment you become their wife they have the handling of your fortune and to all intents and purposes it is theirs."

"I think that is very unfair!" Odela protested.

Her father looked at her in a startled fashion.

"Don't tell me that you are becoming one of these new women who want to have everything in their own hands and no longer wish to rely on their husbands!"

"I think the answer to that is, it depends on the husband," Odela replied,

Her father threw up his hands in horror.

"Now you are really frightening me. And I am told that Her Majesty the Queen is horrified at the sentiments expressed by a number of women who resent obeying their husbands or being dependent on them."

"Even in Florence I have heard about them," Odela told him, "and I promise you, Papa, I will not join them nor, if it upsets you, express any desire to be independent."

"Thank Goodness for that!" the Earl said fervently. "But you have to be very careful indeed."

"Of course I will be," Odela replied, "but promise me, Papa, you will not try to marry me off too quickly. I want to be with you! I want to be with you!"

She smiled at him as she went on,

"And I want to ride with you. And if it is a question of protection, why should I want anybody else but *you*?"

The Earl laughed.

"If you made that sort of speech in the House of Lords, I am sure that their Lordships would appreciate it."

"Nonsense," Odela parried, "they would be horrified, unless I was disguised as a man!"

The Earl laughed again.

Then he said,

"Now what I have planned, my dearest, is that tomorrow, before you become too bogged down with parties and even more parties, you and I will go to see the Solicitors who are handling your grandmother's fortune."

He stopped for a moment and then went on,

"I would expect that they will want you to sign a great number of documents and also I think it right that you should know how much you possess, at the moment."

He paused before the last three words, which made Odela ask,

"Are you saying, Papa, that it is growing."

"Almost every day," her father replied. "In fact to me the whole scenario is nothing less than incredible!"

"It will be interesting to hear about it and then perhaps, Papa, we could build the schools on the estate that Mama wanted as well as a hospital."

"We will certainly consider both," the Earl agreed. "But I would not like your future husband, when you have one, to think that I have extracted money from my daughter that should in fact be his."

"If he thinks like that," Odela said, "then he will not be my future husband. I promise you, Papa. I am going to very very particular – and bear in mind exactly what you have just said to me."

She thought as she spoke that it would be very wrong if her grandmother's fortune, which had come to her mother, should be dissipated on gambling or racing or any of the things in which she knew that a number of Society men had lost their fortunes.

Her father had gone over to his writing desk.

From a drawer he produced the two miniatures that they had talked about previously.

He put them down on the leather blotter, which bore his crest.

Odela thought that both the miniatures were beautifully painted. Her mother's had faded a little with the years, but it still showed her as a beautiful child.

And without being conceited Odela could say the same about her own.

Then her father took out another miniature that had been painted of her mother soon after he had married her.

It was easier to see the striking resemblance between mother and daughter and Odela said,

"I love that miniature and I would love to be able to admire it every day."

"Then that is what you must do," her father said, "so take it, my dearest, and have it with you wherever you go."

Odela gave a little cry.

"Do you mean that, Papa, do you really mean it?"

"I want you to feel that your mother is always with you, guiding you and helping you to use your instinct."

"I shall look at this miniature a dozen times a day and pray every night that she will help me," Odela said.

Her father kissed her.

"When you talk like that, my dearest, I am quite certain that your mother is near to us both," he commented simply.

The way he spoke made the tears come into Odela's eyes.

She picked up the miniature of her mother and held it to her breast.

"Thank you – thank you, Papa!" she said, "you could not give me anything that I am more thrilled to have or that means more to me."

She kissed him again and her father suggested,

"I suppose we should now go and join your stepmother and her friends."

Odela shook her head.

"I have been travelling for a very long time, Papa, and I am very tired. I am sure that Stepmama will forgive me if I go to bed."

"Of course she will," the Earl agreed, "and I will make your apologies."

He then put the two miniatures of his wife and daughter back into the drawer of his writing desk.

Carrying the other miniature in her hand Odela walked beside him down the passage and up the stairs towards the drawing room.

Everywhere she looked there had been changes.

She felt, because so much of what had been so familiar to her had been stripped away, that she was a stranger in. her own home.

She knew, however, that to say so would upset her father.

She slipped her hand into his.

"I love you, Papa," she said, "and please let me spend as much time as possible with you. It is rather frightening meeting – so many strangers."

Her father's fingers tightened on hers.

"I do understand, my dearest, and I promise I will even neglect my duties at the House of Lords for you."

"Then – could we ride early in the morning in Hyde Park?" Odela asked him in a low voice.

Her father gave a short laugh.

"I would like that more than anything. But remember you will be late every night dancing until dawn, so I think you must ask me that question in two or three weeks' time."

"I shall certainly ask it," Odela assured him.

"Then if you do, I will agree," her father promised.

By this time they had reached the door into the drawing room and Odela could hear her stepmother's voice.

She kissed her father.

"Goodnight, my darling daughter," he said. "Sleep very well and we will go out together after luncheon tomorrow."

"I shall be looking forward to it and please make my excuses to Stepmama."

Her father opened the door and Odela had a quick glimpse of her stepmother seated on the sofa before she turned away.

She was glittering with diamonds and looking exceedingly pretty.

She was talking to a man who was seated beside her and Odela wondered vaguely what had happened to the third member of her stepmother's party.

Then because she wanted to escape and be alone she ran to her bedroom.

It was situated at the end of the first floor and was not the room that she had occupied in the past.

That was up another flight of stairs and she wished that she was there, but thought that it would be a mistake to ask for anything special on her first night back.

When she went into the room, she realised that it was a guest room that had been completely refurbished by her stepmother and she wondered if there was any significance in the choice.

Perhaps her stepmother was already planning to be rid of her almost as soon as she arrived,

Then she told herself that she was being unnecessarily suspicious.

The Countess had welcomed her, but she was undoubtedly aware that she had inherited a vast fortune.

'If she enjoys helping me to spend it, she will not wish me to be married too quickly,' Odela reasoned to herself.

It suddenly seemed a logical idea.

Yet something within her told her that what she was thinking was wrong.

"But how can it be?" Odela asked out loud.

There was no answer to her question from anywhere.

CHAPTER TWO

"I am sorry that you went to bed early last night," the Countess was saying.

There was just three of them to luncheon as the Earl and Odela were leaving immediately afterwards.

"I did not wish to seem rude," Odela replied, "but I was very tired after such a long train journey."

"Of course I understood," the Countess said in a cooing voice. "At the same time I would like you to have met the Viscount More who was with me."

She turned to look at her husband as she went on,

"You know that he is the son of your friend the Earl of Morland, Arthur, and I believe almost as intelligent as his father."

"I have never thought that Morland was intelligent," the Earl replied, "and his speeches in the Lords are lamentable!"

The Countess smiled.

"I think, dearest, you are comparing him with yourself and no one can make such brilliant and witty speeches as you manage to do, even on the dullest subjects."

"Now you are flattering me," the Earl started to protest. "But I have to admit that we do have quite a number of extremely prosaic subjects on which it is difficult to be anything but dull!"

Odela laughed.

"I am sure you are being modest, Papa, and all the members of the House of Lords must wish that they could speak like you do."

"Well, John More is a very intelligent young man," the Countess insisted, "and I am sure that he dances well, so I must ask him to some of the dinner parties we give before a ball."

"Oh, please," Odela said, "don't plan too many too quickly. I am sure that it will be some time before my new gowns are ready."

As she spoke, she had the feeling that she was being rushed and pushed into doing something that would turn out to be overwhelming.

It was almost like swimming in a rough sea in which she could not breathe.

"Now don't be nervous, dearest child," her stepmother said, "you know that I will look after you, you will be a huge success and your father will be very proud of you."

Once again Odela had a strong feeling that everything her stepmother said had a special meaning behind it that was not apparent.

'I must be imagining things,' she told herself, as she went upstairs to put on her hat and coat.

But she was becoming more and more sure that there was something in the atmosphere that was definitely menacing.

As she ran down the stairs, she had the feeling that she and her father were escaping.

She could almost see a growing darkness creeping towards them.

'I am being foolish,' Odela chided herself yet again.

But, as her father settled down in the carriage beside her, she slipped her hand into his.

"This is like old times, Papa, to be driving with you," she enthused, "but I wish that we were in the woods in an open chaise."

"We will do it again," the Earl promised. "It's just that this is a bad time of the year for me with Queen Victoria demanding more of my presence than usual and a great number of important bills coming up to the House of Lords from the House of Commons."

"I understand," Odela said, "and this afternoon you are playing truant, so let's enjoy it!"

Her fingers tightened on his as she then asked,

"Tell me about Dragonfly. Have you been riding him since I have been away? Is he jumping as well as he did?"

Her father answered all her questions in detail.

He was an exceptionally good rider and all the horses in his stables were of the finest bloodstock.

By the time they reached the Solicitors Odela was more determined than ever that she would ride with him before breakfast.

After that, she knew, his work for the day began.

At the Solicitors they were greeted respectfully with much bowing and scraping.

She and her father were shown into the rather grand office of the Senior Partner of the Firm and Odela could not help thinking that he was more obsequious to her than he was to her father.

She wondered whether it was because she was so rich.

'That is the sort of thought I should not have!' she told herself severely.

Nevertheless two hours later she realised that she had not been mistaken.

As they drove back to Grosvenor Square, it was difficult for Odela to know what to say.

Never had she imagined in her wildest dreams that she would possess so much money and there was a strong probability of there being a great deal more.

Mr. Hallett, the Senior Partner, had explained to her quite simply about the shares.

When they had been left to her grandmother by her American Godfather, they had been practically worthless.

The Company in which the money had been invested was drilling for oil and the process was proving to be very expensive. And none had been found on their concessions for over a year.

"There was therefore," Mr. Hallett declared, "a possibility that they would go into liquidation and shut down and the documents that your grandmother received from America were just left in the Bank and, I think, forgotten."

Because it sounded such an exciting story, Odela asked him eagerly,

"Then what happened?"

"Nothing until your grandmother died," Mr. Hallett responded, "then the shares were counted among her assets before they were passed on to your mother."

"Mama never mentioned them to me," Odela stated.

She looked at her father as she spoke and he smiled as he said,

"Quite frankly I believed that they were worthless and suspected that the Company had in fact gone into liquidation."

"Then after your mother's death," Mr. Hallett went on, "in assessing her assets the shares were remembered and we made enquiries."

He looked at the Earl as he added,

"In fact, my Lord, on your instructions, you may well recall, we wrote to America to find out what the situation was."

"I admit," the Earl said, "that I thought that it was really a waste of time and postage!"

Mr. Hallett smiled.

"Then when we received a reply after some delay, it was a shock to us and a considerable one to your Lordship."

"I was astounded," the Earl agreed.

He looked at Odela as he said,

"You had already left for Florence, my dear, and there was no reason to tell you what we had discovered while you were so far away."

"I don't think I would have believed you," Odela replied. "It all sounds too fantastic to be true!"

"That is what my Partner and I thought," Mr. Hallett said, "and, as your Lordship now realises, in the last year the shares have doubled in price and there is every likelihood of them doing so again and yet again."

He looked down at some papers in front of him and suggested,

"I think, my Lady, you should see exactly what your holding in this company is worth at this particular moment."

He passed the papers across the desk to Odela, who just stared at the figures thinking that they made no sense.

Now in the carriage she said to her father in a voice that was rather frightened,

"What can we do with so much money, Papa?"

"The first thing," the Earl replied, "is to keep quiet about it. The fewer people who know how rich you are the better."

"That is what I would want, but people will always gossip."

She was thinking of her stepmother.

The Countess would want to tell her special friends and they would tell their friends and there would be no chance then of anybody not being aware that she was a considerable heiress.

Impulsively she turned to her father.

"Please, Papa, make Stepmama promise that she will tell no one about all this money and how rich I am."

"I have already told Esme that it must be kept a secret," the Earl replied.

He did not, however, speak very positively and Odela had the feeling that he was well aware that his wife would talk.

She would also wish to have the pleasure of producing a girl who her friends would pay special attention to.

They drove on and, after what seemed a long silence, Odela said,

"It's a great responsibility, Papa, and you will have to help me."

"You know I will," her father answered, "and don't let it worry you, my dearest. You have only just come home."

He paused a moment and then went on,

"When you are more settled, we will talk about spending it in some of the ways that would have pleased your mother."

"If I can do that, I will not be so frightened of it," Odela murmured.

"You are a very sensible child," the Earl said approvingly.

They were nearing Grosvenor Square and he looked at his watch.

"I am already late for the House of Lords," he said. "Now what I would like you to do, my dearest, is to take these papers up to my bedroom and put them in the top drawer of my dressing table."

Odela knew that it was the chest of drawers on the top of which he placed his ivory hairbrushes and above it hung a very fine George III mirror.

"I would like you to do that," the Earl went on, "because I don't want anybody in the house, including my secretary, to see them. When I return I will put them all in my safe."

He had a private safe in his bedroom where he kept his money and the family jewels.

"I will do that, Papa," Odela agreed, "but please don't let anyone see them."

She was thinking of her stepmother as she spoke and, as if he understood, the Earl said,

"I promise you that they shall be kept from all prying eyes."

As he spoke, the horses drew up outside Shalford House and Odela kissed him.

"Thank you, Papa," she sighed, "and please come back early if you can."

"I will do my best," the Earl promised, "but unfortunately some of my fellow Peers are very long winded!"

Odela laughed and, as the footman opened the carriage door, she stepped out.

She stood on the pavement and waved until her father had driven away.

Then carrying the papers in her hand she walked into the house.

She was afraid that she might encounter her stepmother who would insist on seeing what she was carrying.

She therefore ran quickly up the stairs and along the passage to her father's bedroom.

It was large and impressive and like most of the best bedrooms it overlooked the gardens in the square.

There was no valet on duty there at this time of the day and Odela carefully closed the door behind her before she crossed the room to her father's dressing table.

She pulled open the drawer.

It contained quite a number of other papers, some loose sovereigns and a few pieces of silver. There were a number of jewel boxes as well and she knew that they contained his cufflinks, his evening waistcoat buttons and the pearl studs he wore in his dress shirt.

She put the papers at the back of the drawer just in case his valet should disturb them.

Then she closed it and walked to the fireplace to look up at the portrait that hung over it.

It was a very beautiful portrait of her mother, which had been painted the year that she was married.

Odela thought it looked very much as she did now.

The Countess had been eighteen when she married and nineteen when Odela was born.

She had fair hair and a pink-and-white skin and her large eyes were the soft grey of a pigeon's breast and were exceedingly beautiful.

She also looked ethereal and, as her father had said, Odela could feel her spirituality.

"If only you were here, Mama," she said aloud, looking up at the portrait. "It would be such fun doing things with you. Now you could build your hospital, open your schools and help so many people as you always wanted to do."

As Odela finished speaking, she felt that her mother was telling her that was what she must do.

"I will – try, Mama – I will really try," Odela promised, "but – you will have to – help me."

She felt the tears come into her eyes again and almost impatiently she turned away from the picture.

She had cried for so long and so bitterly when her mother had died and it was Nanny who had said to her firmly,

"Now, dearie, you stop upsettin' your mother as you're doin' right now."

Odela had stared at her as Nanny went on,

"Of course you're upsettin' her! And what do you expect when you cry like that and don't eat. You're makin' everybody else miserable as well!"

"Do you – really think – Mama can – see me?" Odela asked.

"Of course she can see you," Nanny replied, "and if you asks me, she's ashamed of you when you should be helpin' your poor father!"

Nanny had spoken in a scolding voice, but Odela felt that she had brought a light into the darkness that surrounded her.

She had stopped crying.

When her father came home, looking far older than he actually was, she had done everything she could to interest and amuse him.

In some respects she had succeeded.

It gave her a warm feeling in her heart to think that her mother was pleased with her.

She was sure that Nanny was right in saying that her mother could see and hear the people she most loved – her husband and her daughter.

'I will – not cry,' Odela vowed to herself, 'but I miss Mama more than I ever have done before.'

She was just about to leave the room when to her surprise she heard voices and for a moment she could not imagine where they came from.

Then she was aware that the sound came from the communicating door that led into what had been her mother's boudoir.

The main bedrooms in the house all had communicating doors into an adjacent dressing room.

These were used by a husband if his wife was sleeping in the bedroom.

But in the Master suite her father's room was at the end of the passage.

Next to it was the boudoir and beyond that there was her mother's bedroom also with a connecting door.

Odela remembered now that her stepmother had changed the boudoir into a sitting room.

The connecting door must have been left ajar and Odela thought that she ought to close it as it might be a mistake for her father's valet to overhear what was being said,

She went to the door and was just about to push it when she heard her stepmother saying,

"She is already a millionairess and the money is increasing day by day, if not hour by hour!"

Odela drew in her breath.

As she had earlier suspected, her stepmother was already talking about her fortune.

Then a man's voice replied,

"I am not interested, Esme, in your stepdaughter, as you well know, but in you!"

"That is very sweet of you to say so," the Countess answered, "and, of course, it is what I want you to feel. At the same time, Johnny darling, you must realise that this is an opportunity you cannot miss!"

Odela stood as if transfixed.

She knew now who her stepmother was talking to.

It was the Viscount More she had spoken about at luncheontime.

"Why, oh, why," the Viscount now exclaimed, "did I not meet you before you married Shalford!"

"You were in India being a brave soldier," the Countess replied, "and before that I was married to Herbert."

"You were a widow for a whole year," the Viscount groaned, "before Fate brought us together."

"Fate is sometimes very cruel," the Countess said with what sounded like a little sob in her voice. "Equally you know as well as I do that you could not afford a wife then, any more than you can now."

"Things will be different when my father dies," the Viscount remarked.

"Very little," the Countess said. "If you are honest, my dearest, you know that your father is not a wealthy man by any means and your house needs thousands of pounds spent on it."

"That is true," the Viscount admitted, "but I want you, Esme! I want you unbearably!"

"As I want you," the Countess replied softly. "That is why you have to listen to what I have to say."

"All I want is to be near you, to talk to you and to make love to you."

"And all that will be possible," the Countess whispered softly, "if you marry Odela."

"What do I want with an unfledged girl of eighteen?" the Viscount asked roughly. "I want you as I have never wanted any woman before."

There was a silence during which Odela was sure that the Viscount was kissing her stepmother.

She was aware that she was eavesdropping on them and it was something that she knew she should not stoop to do.

At the same time she had to hear clearly what her stepmother was planning.

It seemed a long time before the Countess said in a voice that was a little unsteady,

"Oh, darling, you know I adore you, but we have to be practical and we also have to be very very careful."

"I know that," the Viscount said, "but all I want to do is to carry you away to some desert island where we can be alone and not be afraid of every eye that looks at us and every ear that hears what we are saying."

"It would be wonderful, absolutely wonderful, to be anywhere with you," the Countess said almost in a whisper.

Then in a different tone of voice she added,

"And we *can* be together, if you will do as I say."

"You mean – marry your stepdaughter!"

"I mean that because it will open the way for us to be together without anyone being able to question it."

The Viscount .did not speak and the Countess went on,

"You will, Johnny darling, have unlimited money at your disposal. The first thing will be to buy a house in London as near to this one as possible. Odela will wish to be near her father and you and I will be able to see each other all the time."

"With your husband and my wife watching us?" the Viscount asked.

"If we are clever, why should they have the slightest suspicion that I love you?" the Countess asked.

"As I love you," the Viscount murmured.

"Also," the Countess resumed, "until you come into your own ancestral home, I will persuade Arthur to lend you the Dower House."

She gave a little laugh before she said,

"Odela prefers the country and she will be quite happy to spend a great deal of time there. Then with her money you can buy anything in the world you want."

The Countess's voice rose a little as she added,

"Think of it, Johnny, a yacht that we can all journey in to foreign parts. Racehorses that will take us to all the smartest Meetings!"

She paused before she said, almost as an aside,

"Arthur hates racing and I don't think that Odela cares for it either."

Still the Viscount was silent until she said,

"Oh, Johnny, think of the possibilities! I shall so enjoy helping you do all the things you have wanted to do and which you never had enough money for."

At last the Viscount found his voice.

"You are making it all sound very easy, Esme," he said. "But you know as well as I do that women are jealous and Odela may have very strong ideas about being permanently in the company of her stepmother, especially when she is as beautiful as you."

"It is angelic of you to say I am beautiful," the Countess said in her cooing voice, "but Odela is very young and, as she loves her father, she will want to be with him."

She smiled at him before she went on,

"An older woman would not cling to him in the same manner. Also you have forgotten something."

"What is that?" the Viscount asked.

"You want an heir and nothing ties a woman to the house more than children!"

"You are very plausible, Esme," the Viscount declared slowly. "But if I have an heir, which, of course, is imperative at some time, I would want it to be your son and mine."

There was a definite pause before the Countess responded to him,

"And, of course, if it was possible, that would be completely blissful. But, as I have been telling you, Johnny darling, we have to make the best of what we can do and, if you are brave enough, *will* do."

"It is not a question of being brave enough," the Earl said sulkily, "but of having another woman in my arms instead of you. Do you know how much I adore you?"

He spoke harshly.

"As I love you, my strong, handsome marvellous lover," Esme sighed, "And that is why I cannot lose you."

"You will never lose me," the Viscount said passionately. "I would go down to Hell itself rather than that!"

He was kissing her again.

As if she awoke from a dream, Odela moved away.

She walked towards the door that led into the passage and, when she reached it, she looked back at her mother's portrait over the mantelpiece.

There was a stricken look in her eyes as she did so.

Then she opened the door quietly and let herself out of her father's bedroom.

She ran to her own room and, finding it empty, locked the door.

She threw herself down on the bed, she was not crying but thinking.

Now she knew why, ever since she had come back, she had not only felt that there was something wrong but also that she was being menaced.

It was as if what her stepmother was plotting and planning had conveyed itself to her.

Somehow she *must* escape.

Instead of feeling hysterical or that she must cry, however, she suddenly felt cool and detached.

It was as if she was struggling to learn a complicated subject. Or trying to find the solution to a mathematical problem.

There was one thing that she was sincerely grateful for and which she felt was Fate.

It was that she now knew where her enemy lay.

'I cannot be taken by surprise,' she murmured to herself.

It was almost as if she was reading a book and the plot was unfolding before her eyes.

She could guess exactly how her stepmother would connive to ensure that she was married to the Viscount.

To begin with her father was a friend of his father.

Secondly, if the Viscount had been a soldier her father could not accuse him of being a 'waster'. Nor could he say that he hung about gambling in Clubs.

She had the idea that he was older than the usual young man who she would be introduced to at balls.

Her stepmother, she knew, was twenty-seven and the Viscount would doubtless be either the same age or older.

'Papa will be convinced that he is at the right age to handle my money sensibly,' Odela thought, 'also to protect and look after me.'

The horror of being married to a man who loved another woman, especially when it was her stepmother, swept over her.

She recognised that it was degrading and shameful that the Countess should be unfaithful to her father.

At the same time it was appalling that she was planning that her lover should marry her stepdaughter for her money.

'It is something that will never happen,' Odela vowed to herself.

Yet she realised that she would have to be very clever not to be caught in the trap that was being set for her.

Because she loved her father she could not tell him what she had overheard.

Although he obviously still loved her mother, he was both infatuated with and very attracted to his new wife.

Odela knew by the expression in his eyes that he appreciated her beauty and, when Esme flattered and touched him, he was as pleased as any man would have been.

'How can I destroy Papa?' she asked.

If she was honest, she felt that he had been happier since he had married for the second time.

He had been lost and lonely after her mother died and Esme was very astute in the way that she made him feel important to her.

'Of course,' Odela then told herself, 'I could always tell Papa that I have taken an overwhelming dislike to the Viscount and could not bear in any circumstances to be his wife.'

It was unfortunately not just a question of having only her father to reckon with.

He would not have forced her into a marriage that she did not want.

But she was aware of how subtly her stepmother handled him.

Somehow Esme would persuade him that the Viscount was the one man in London who was not a fortune-hunter and she would be very plausible in saying that love would come after marriage.

There was something else that Odela reasoned.

If her stepmother could marry her off quickly to the Viscount, there would then be no other men who she could choose a husband from.

'She will make sure of that,' Odela thought, 'by telling her friends that the Viscount is in love with me and that I am in love with him. It would soon be known to the other men I meet at dances that I am already secretly engaged.'

She could see it all happening, as if it was a play being enacted before her very eyes.

"What – can I – do? Oh, – God, what can – I do?" she called out aloud.

She thought that her voice sounded desperate and knew that she had to act quickly to save herself.

She looked at the miniature of her mother and picked it up in her hands.

'Help me – Mama,' she whispered, 'help me – otherwise I shall be lost.'

She thought as she said the words that her stepmother, like a dark malevolent witch, was standing over her.

She was willing her, forcing her by supernatural means into a marriage that would mean a life of misery and despair for her.

'It's your money, Mama,' she went on gazing to the miniature, 'and therefore you must either make it vanish – or I – must!'

As she spoke, she knew that there was a solution.

She must go away at least for the moment.

She must escape from the trap that was closing in on her and, if she did not hurry, it might be too late.

She walked to the window, still holding the miniature in her hand.

The sun was sinking, but it was still shining on the garden in the centre of the square.

The fountain was throwing its water high towards the sky and then it fell sparkling and iridescent like a rainbow.

The flowerbeds in the square were filled with tulips all crimson and yellow and the leaves of the trees were the pale green of the spring.

'I will go to the country,' Odela said to herself. 'At least I shall be able to think there.'

She thought of Dragonfly.

If she could ride him through the woods as she had done so often, she was sure that somehow she could find a way out of her predicament.

'It's like facing a very high fence,' she told herself. 'If Dragonfly and I can jump it, then I shall find a way of escape on the other side.'

She sighed.

'If only there was someone I could talk to, someone who would understand what I am feeling.'

It was then, almost like a message from her mother, that she remembered Nanny.

Nanny would understand.

Nanny with the wisdom of years might even have the answers for her.

'I will go to Nanny,' she decided there and then.

Now she knew that she was no longer as frightened as she had been before and it was then once again that her brain became cool and she could think clearly.

She unlocked the door and rang the bell for a maid.

The servants she had seen since she came home were all strangers to her and they were obviously not particularly interested in her needs.

After some delay the door opened and it was an older woman who looked at her somewhat coldly.

"You rang, my Lady?"

"Yes, Jones," Odela replied. "I want to ask you if there is anyone in the house who was here before I went abroad."

"I don't think there is, my Lady – " Jones began.

Then she stopped.

" – that is, unless your Ladyship remembers Miss Gatesly."

Odela gave a little cry.

"Miss Gatesly, the seamstress? Is she still here?"

"Yes, my Lady. We've found her ever so skilful with the linen and she's even done some alterations to her Ladyship's gowns."

"Ask Miss Gatesly to come to see me at once," Odela ordered.

"Very good, my Lady."

Jones left and Odela thought with a little warmth in her heart that 'Gatesy', as she had called her as a child, was exactly who she wanted at this moment.

It was not long before the seamstress appeared.

She was now over sixty and the rheumatism in her legs prevented her from moving as quickly as she once had.

She was now smiling with delight at seeing Odela.

As she came into the room, Odela ran towards her.

"Gatesy!" she cried. "I had no idea that you were still here."

"I were hopin' to see you, my Lady," Miss Gatesly said, "but I didn't want to intrude when you'd only just come back from foreign parts."

Odela drew her into the room and closed the door behind her.

"Now listen, Gatesy," she said, "I need your help and I need it desperately!"

CHAPTER THREE

The train moved out of Paddington Station.

Odela sat back in her seat and thought that things had gone far better than she had dared to hope.

When Gatesy had come into her room looking, she thought, very much the same as when she was a child, she had run forward to kiss her.

"Gatesy!" she exclaimed, "I had no idea that you were still in the house. Everybody else is a stranger."

"Her Ladyship kept me on as she finds me useful," Gatesy replied, "but it's so good to see you, my Lady, 'tis indeed."

"And I need you desperately," Odela repeated.

She drew Gatesy by the hand across the room to where there were two comfortable armchairs near the window.

"Now sit down," Odela suggested, "and first of all, tell me how you are."

"I'm gettin' old," Gatesy replied, "and I'd like to retire, but her Ladyship intimated that if I did I'd get no pension."

Odela stiffened.

"Of course you will have a pension!" she cried, "and you can retire at once if you want to. I will see to that."

She knew by the expression in Gatesy's eyes that she was aware she had money.

"I suppose you have heard," Odela said, "that Mama left me some money?"

"They've been talkin' about it in the housekeeper's room," Gatesy told her, "and I'm right glad for you, my Lady, I am that."

"So am I, Gatesy, but something else has happened and I have to go to the country immediately."

She paused for a moment before she continued,

"I will be frank, Gatesy, and tell you that I have to escape. And I want you to come with me."

Odela had the feeling without her explaining it that Gatesy understood.

Nothing went on in the house that was not known and talked about in the housekeeper's room and doubtless they knew already that her stepmother intended to marry her off to the Viscount.

And they would be very well aware of what his position was.

She thought, however, that there was no need to go into details where Gatesy was concerned.

Instead she said,

"I have to leave secretly or both Papa and my stepmother will stop me."

"Secretly!" Gatesy exclaimed. "How, my Lady, can you do that?"

"It will be quite easy if you will help me," Odela replied, "because I know that I should not travel alone."

"I should think not indeed!" Gatesy exclaimed, "you're far too young and pretty."

"What I want you to do," Odela went on, "is to creep out very early in the morning before anybody else is awake."

She paused for a moment and dropped her voice.

"I am sure there is a train from Paddington going to Oxford and I will somehow find out the actual time."

"Mr. Bennett has a timetable in his office," Gatesy then informed her.

Mr. Bennett was the Earl's secretary.

"You are already being very helpful," Odela told her, "and I will let you know exactly what time we will leave."

She paused before she added,

"What I want you to do is to tell everybody in the house early in the morning, when only the footmen and the lower housemaids are up, that a relative of yours is ill and you need a Hackney carriage to take you to the Station."

"I'll do that," Gatesy nodded.

"You will drive away with the luggage," Odela went on, "and I will leave the house by the garden door. Tell the coachman to stop at the top of the Mews where you are picking up a friend."

She stopped to think for a moment and then resumed,

"No one will think for a moment it is me until later in the day when Papa finds my letter telling him that I have gone away to stay with friends."

She repeated this several times so that Gatesy had it all firmly in her head.

Then the older woman asked,

"I suppose you've got some money, my Lady? I've not been paid yet this month."

"I have plenty of money and as soon as we are home I will talk to the Estate Manager and see that he gives you a cottage, if possible one that does not belong to Papa. Then there can be no argument about it."

She saw tears coming into Gatesy's eyes.

"You're ever so kind, my Lady," she said, "just like your dear mother before you. I've been so worried about meself, seein' that I've rheumatism in my hands."

"I promise you one thing," Odela stated. "You shall spend your retirement in real comfort and there will be nothing that my stepmother can do about it."

She could not disguise the bitter note in her voice, but Gatesy did not look surprised.

She merely said,

"Her Ladyship'll be real angry if she finds out that I've gone away with you."

"When she does know, it will be too late," Odela asserted.

When Gatesy had left her, Odela sat planning every move she would now make.

It was nearly dinnertime before her stepmother realised that she was in the house.

She came to Odela's bedroom door just as the maids were bringing in her bath to set down in front of the fire.

"Oh, here you are, dear child," the Countess said in her most gushing tones. "I wondered where you could be."

"When I came in, I was told that you were entertaining visitors," Odela answered, "so I did not like to disturb you."

"That was very sweet of you," the Countess cooed, "but I wish I had known."

She paused for a moment before she carried on,

"Wear one of your prettiest gowns this evening, as we are having a smart dinner party and I have placed you next to the Viscount More who I know you will find most interesting."

She gave one of her tinkling little laughs.

"I think he is as fond of horses as you are!"

Odela did not reply and her stepmother went to her own room.

After what she had said Odela wanted to choose the ugliest gown that she possessed.

Unfortunately everything she had bought in Florence was in perfect taste and each gown made her look more attractive than the last.

Finally she told herself that, if she was to act the part that was expected of her, all she had to do was to look pretty and say nothing.

She went into the drawing room before dinner.

She found her stepmother embellished with jewels and looking, she had to admit, extremely attractive.

Odela remembered one of the girls at school saying once,

"My father always says that every woman looks beautiful when she is in love."

Odela thought scornfully that was what her stepmother was, but not to the man she was married to.

When the Viscount came into the room, she knew at once that he was a man for whom she could never have any affection let alone love.

He was indeed good-looking, but she thought that there was something ineffectual about him.

She was quite certain that he would never make a Politician. Nor would he strive to do anything positive in his life.

'Except of course,' she added to herself, 'make love to – another man's wife!'

She was aware that the Viscount on her stepmother's orders was trying to make himself extremely pleasant to her.

At the same time, when he was off his guard, he was gazing at her stepmother.

Odela thought that anyone who was particularly observant would guess where his true feelings lay and she wondered if her father had noticed the glances that passed between his wife and the Viscount.

Then she recalled reading somewhere that the *'husband was always the last one to know'* as well, she added, the last to believe that the woman in whom he trusted was unfaithful.

She glanced down the table to see that her father was looking happy.

She knew it was because the women on either side of him were not only beautiful but also intelligent.

They were both making him laugh and he was being, Odela knew, witty and amusing, as he used to be when her mother was alive.

'I cannot make him unhappy by telling him what is going on behind his back,' she told herself again.

She recognised that it would be an exceedingly cruel thing to do to him.

When the ladies left the dining room, leaving the gentlemen to their port, Odela hurried upstairs.

She knew that at this moment her father's room would be empty and his valet would be, as he called it, 'givin' a hand' in the pantry.

She went into the bedroom and locked the door.

She knew where her father kept the key of the safe.

He had fondly believed in the past that it was known only to her mother, but Odela had often helped her mother take the jewels out of the safe that she wished to wear that evening.

She therefore went to the secret hiding place to find that the key was indeed there.

She unlocked the safe and, as she had expected, she could see the papers that they had brought away from the Solicitors. They had already been placed there by her father.

The top shelf contained papers and the next contained money.

He always kept some handy in case it was necessary for him to have ready cash for an urgent payment.

She took out quite a number of banknotes and also some sovereigns.

Then she replaced the key and went to her own bedroom.

The ladies were all tidying themselves in her stepmother's room and quickly Odela went down the stairs so that she was in the drawing room before they returned.

When dinner was over, the Viscount came obediently to her side and he tried to engage her in a conversation about horses.

She responded to him for several minutes and then went to the piano saying,

"I feel sure that it will brighten up the party if I play to them."

A little later her father told her how delighted he was that she played so well.

"It is all due to you, Papa," she replied. "You paid for the most expensive music teacher in Florence."

"My money was obviously well spent," her father smiled, "but I feel that you should be talking to our guests."

"I want you to hear two more pieces I have learnt," Odela answered and he did not press her.

She went to bed at the first opportunity, knowing that she had a great deal to do.

Gatesy had managed to bring to her room a small trunk that was not too heavy.

She had hidden it in one of the cupboards and Odela packed into it her best gowns and, of course, her riding clothes.

Then, after her stepmother had retired to bed, the night footman knocked on her door.

Odela opened it.

"Miss Gatesly tells me, my Lady," he said, "there be a trunk as contains some things you're givin' her."

"Yes, of course, and they are all ready," Odela replied to him in a low voice, "but I did not think Miss Gatesly would want them this evening."

"Miss Gatesly tells me she has to leave early in the mornin'," the footman replied. "She's had bad news."

"I am sorry about that," Odela said, "and what a good thing the clothes I am giving her are ready."

The footman carried off the trunk and Odela undressed and climbed into bed.

She was used to rising early as in Florence the pupils who had special tuition often had to begin their lessons at seven o'clock promptly

She was therefore ready and dressed by ten minutes to six. She had learnt from the timetable in the secretary's office that there was a train from Paddington to Oxford at six-thirty.

She and Gatesy caught it quite easily after she had climbed into the Hackney carriage at the top of the Mews.

Odela had written a letter to her father, which she had carefully put on his writing desk in his study.

She knew that he would not go to his desk until after breakfast.

In it she wrote,

"My Dearest Papa,

I am so stunned and upset by my huge fortune I learnt about yesterday that I feel I need time to think.

I know you will understand that it is impossible to do so in London with so many engagements and so many things to buy.

I am therefore going to the country for a few days so that I can ride Dragonfly and sort things out in my own mind.

I know you would not approve of me travelling alone, so I am taking Miss Gatesly with me.

*I have also borrowed some money from your safe
and I will, of course, pay you back!!!"*

Odela had added a number of exclamation marks
after the last word so that her father would realise that
she was making a joke.

Then she ended her letter,

*"I love you, Papa, and I want to spend my
fortune exactly as you and Mama would want me to
do, but I really do have to think very carefully about
it.*

*Please don't be angry with me and let me have
just a little time to myself.*

*Your very loving and affectionate daughter,
Odela."*

She felt that her father would understand.

At the same time she was absolutely certain that
her stepmother would not.

'She will try to force me back,' she thought, 'and
then I shall be in her power.'

Every instinct in her body had told her last night
how dangerous the situation now was.

She only had to look round the house to realise
the changes that had been made and, behind every
change and the smooth-running perfection of it all,
was a strong personality.

There was *nothing* soft, gentle or sweet about her
stepmother.

She was a woman who was determined to have her own way and would move Heaven and Earth to get it.

It would not concern her if anyone was hurt in the process.

'The Viscount has already agreed to what she has suggested,' Odela murmured to herself, 'and unless I am fully on my guard I shall wake up to find myself married to him almost before I can breathe!'

"You're lookin' ever so worried, my Lady," Gatesy ventured from the other side of the carriage.

"I am really very happy that we got away so easily," Odela replied to her.

She knew it was because they had started so early as she had learned that her stepmother was never called until ten o'clock in the morning.

When they arrived in Oxford, it was not difficult to hire a carriage to take them the five miles to Shalford Hall, which was deep in the countryside.

The moment they were clear of the beautiful City of Oxford with its spires and towers, Odela began to feel different.

This was the England she knew and loved with its woods, its hills and silver rivers.

As soon as the carriage drew to a standstill outside The Hall, Odela jumped out.

She hurried up the steps to knock on the huge door herself.

When it was opened by a footman, who had been at The Hall since he was a boy, Odela held out her hand.

"James!" she exclaimed. "I was hoping you would still be here."

"Why, if it isn't 'er Ladyship!" the footman cried with obvious pleasure. "I 'eard as you was a-comin' back to England."

"I am back and now – I have come home," Odela replied.

She said the same to the old butler who came hurrying towards her from the pantry.

"We were wonderin' when we'd see you, my Lady," he said, "but we thinks you'd be too busy with all the gaieties in London for us here!"

"All I have wanted – is to come home," Odela said softly.

She did not waste any more time talking.

Leaving the butler to pay the Hackney carriage and look after Gatesy, she ran straight to the stables.

The grooms all greeted her with delight.

But it was Dragonfly she wanted to see more than anything else.

He whinnied when he heard her voice and a few seconds later the stable door was opened and her arms were round him.

"I have missed you! I missed you!" she cried, "Oh, darling Dragonfly, have they looked after you properly? You have not – forgotten me?"

It was very obvious that he had not done so.

He was as delighted to see her as she was to see him.

Odela asked for him to be saddled in an hour and then she took Robinson, the Head Groom, on one side.

It was he who had taught her to ride when she was a very small girl.

She told him that she wanted his help, but when she told him why, he looked worried.

"I have run away from London, Robinson," she began, "and I am going to hide – so that no one will find me for some time."

"Now what you wanna go and do a thing like that for, my Lady?" he asked. "T'aint right. It'll upset 'er Ladyship."

"I realise that," Odela replied, "but it is something I have to do – and I shall need your help to do it."

She thought that Robinson was going to be difficult and said swiftly,

"If you want the truth, her Ladyship wants me to marry somebody for whom I have no liking and – who would make me very unhappy."

She knew by his expression on his face that he had no liking for her stepmother.

"That not be right, my Lady, seein' as you've bin in foreign parts for so long."

"I know, Robinson, but you know what her Ladyship is like – and she will not listen to anything I say."

Robinson pressed his lips together.

"What do you want me to do, my Lady?" he asked. "I've known you all your life and I'll not 'ave you un'appy. I'd cut orf me leg first!"

"I should be very very unhappy if I did what her Ladyship requires," Odela murmured.

After that he agreed to everything she wanted.

It was he who took her over to Nanny's house, promising that if there were any enquiries made he would say that he had no idea where she had gone.

"I hate asking you – to lie, Robinson," she said, "but it will be a little time before her Ladyship insists on my returning to London and – things may have changed by then."

She gave a sigh before she went on,

"But I have to hide somewhere and I know I shall be safe with Nanny."

"'Course you will," Robinson replied stoutly, "and I'll do what you say, my Lady. But when 'is Lordship finds out the truth, 'e might give me me notice!"

"If he does, I swear I will employ you myself and build up my own stable," Odela said impulsively.

She saw the expression of surprise on Robinson's face. He at any rate had not heard about her fortune.

"I have learnt since I returned to England that Mama left me some money, so I promise you,

Robinson, that nobody who served us when Mama was alive will ever need to worry about their future or be without work or money."

Robinson said nothing and Odela went on,

"But please don't talk about it yet, although doubtless you will be hearing about it later."

"You can trust me, my Lady," Robinson assured her.

Having told him exactly what she wanted Odela then went back to the house.

Luncheon was waiting for her and the old butler told her that she had caught them by surprise and there would be a better meal at dinner.

"Mrs. Banks wants to tell you she's done her best," he smiled.

There were so many people who wanted to see Odela.

She therefore decided that it would be a mistake to go to Nanny until the following morning.

She knew exactly where she was living as she had written to her all the time that she had been away at school in Florence.

At first, after she had been dismissed, she had taken a position looking after an Ambassador's children.

But she had not been happy in London, as Odela might have expected, and then six months ago she had left the Embassy.

She had been asked by the sister of the Marquis of Trancombe to look after her small daughter while she went abroad with her husband.

The Marquis of Trancombe's house and estate were only about six miles from Shalford Hall and Odela could understand how delighted Nanny was at the idea of going back to a part of the country that she knew so well.

Odela vaguely remembered the last Marquis when he was a very old man.

He had been a friend of her father and mother and they had often talked about him.

She thought once when she had been small that she had been invited to a children's party at Coombe Court.

The Marquis's son who had now inherited, so far as she could remember, had not been there at the time and later he had gone abroad with his Regiment almost as soon as he left Oxford University.

Nanny had written enthusiastically about Coombe Court.

She said it was a very comfortable impressive house and the nurseries were exactly what she liked.

She wrote,

"I like having the little girl all to myself with no one to interfere. She makes me think of you when you were the same age and how sweet you were."

"We will ride over to see Nanny first thing in the morning," Odela had told Robinson, "and no one but you must know what we are doing."

Because they were riding, the clothes she wanted to take with her had to be put into saddlebags.

Robinson brought the saddlebags to her and she packed the clothes herself.

No one had seen her take them upstairs and they were the deep bags that were usually used for game in the shooting season.

They were able to hold practically everything that she had brought with her from London.

She carefully wrapped up the miniature of her mother and one or two other things that she greatly treasured to carry with her on Dragonfly.

One thing that made it easier was that nearly all the staff at Shalford Hall were old as the younger servants had been taken by her stepmother to London.

They would be brought back again if and when they moved to the country.

The housemaids who had been there for many years moved slowly, but it was not difficult for Odela to carry the saddlebags downstairs herself.

She put them just outside the garden door where no one could see them before Robinson collected them.

She had eaten an early breakfast and then she told the butler and the footmen who were waiting on her that she was going riding.

They were not at all surprised when she walked to the stables rather than have the horses brought round to the front door.

She and Robinson left the stable yard by the back entrance and only two of the stable lads saw them go.

They were far too frightened of Robinson to ask any awkward questions.

Robinson was riding a large stallion that was extremely sturdy and could carry any amount of weight.

Dragonfly was rather skittish, but Odela was sure that he was feeling happy to have her on his back again.

When they were well on their way and had galloped over several green fields, Odela exclaimed,

"It's so wonderful to be back! I cannot tell you how much I have missed being here when I was abroad."

"And we missed you, my Lady," Robinson answered. "T'weren't the same without you comin' and goin' in the stables at all hours!"

"And now I am riding Dragonfly again."

She thought as she was speaking that she would like to ride away into the horizon and never come back.

Then there would be no problems, no Viscount waiting to trap her and no scheming stepmother like a witch stirring up trouble.

Aloud she said,

"Have you seen anything of Nanny since she went to Coombe Court?"

"She's bin in touch with Mrs. Field," Robinson replied, "and told 'er that she's right 'appy there."

Mrs. Field was the housekeeper at The Hall and Odela knew that she must warn Nanny not to let Mrs. Field know who was with her.

"'Ow long does your Ladyship think you'll be a-stayin' at Coombe Court?" Robinson asked in his slow voice.

"I have no idea," Odela answered. "All I want you to do is to say that you don't know where I went when I left home except I told you that I was staying with friends."

"Well, there be a number of 'ouses round abouts where you'd be very welcome, my Lady."

Odela was aware of this and it was lucky, she thought, that Nanny had gone to one whose owner she had never met.

Both his parents, who had known her mother and father, were dead and there had been children with whom she had played ever since she could walk.

Her mother had been very conscious that she was an only child and must therefore have companions of her own age.

Fortunately Oxfordshire was fashionable and boasted a good number of noble and County families.

'If Stepmama visits everybody we know in the hope of finding me, she is going to be busy,' Odela reflected with delight.

It took them less time cross-country to reach the house belonging to the Marquis of Trancombe than if they had travelled by carriage.

It was in an even more beautiful part of the country, Odela thought, than her own home.

There were great woods rising on undulating land and there were exquisite views over meadows filled with the flowers of spring.

Yellow buttercups, forget-me-nots and cuckoo pint all made the fields that they were riding through a glorious picture of nature at its finest.

It was even more beautiful to Odela than any of the famous pictures that she had seen in the Galleries of Florence.

"I am home! *I am home!*" she wanted to cry to the birds, the butterflies and the bees that hovered over the flowers.

Then she remembered that her real home was Shalford Hall.

But if she stayed at The Hall her stepmother would be waiting to carry her off to London and the dreadful Viscount.

It was a thought that made her shiver and she was silent for the last miles before they reached Coombe Court.

When she saw the house in the distance, she gave a little gasp.

With the sun shining on its windows and the statues that decorated its roofs silhouetted against the sky it looked just like a Fairy Castle.

'No wonder Nanny likes living here,' she thought.

There were green lawns sloping down to a huge lake and, as they crossed the bridge that spanned it, Odela could see several swans moving on its silvery surface accompanied by their baby cygnets.

The gardens were filled with flowers and the lilac trees were in full blossom.

Beyond the garden there was an orchard where the fruit trees, pink and white with blossom, transformed it into a magical Wonderland.

Then she remembered that she was supposed to be in hiding and she and Robinson went round the back to the kitchen door.

Robinson knocked.

Odela quickly dismounted saying in case he made a mistake to the kitchenmaid who opened it,

"I have come to visit – Miss West."

"She be upstairs in the nursery," the kitchenmaid answered.

"Would you be very kind and show me the way?" Odela asked her.

She had already arranged that while she was doing this, Robinson would ask the grooms to stable Dragonfly.

"Say I am a relative of Miss West's," she had said to him, "and don't forget that I am called 'Miss West' as well."

"I'll do that, my Lady," Robinson replied.

The kitchenmaid then took Odela up the backstairs to the second floor of the house.

She knocked on a door and, as she opened it, called out,

"Someone to see you, Nanny."

Odela walked in.

Nanny was sitting at a table in the centre of the room sewing and on the floor beside her was a small child playing with some coloured bricks.

For a moment Nanny just stared at her.

Then with a murmur of delight she rose to her feet.

Odela ran forward and flung her arms around her neck.

"Nanny! Oh, Nanny! I am here! Say you are pleased to see me."

"I was hopin' you'd come," Nanny said, "but I thought you'd give me warnin'."

"There was no time for that and I have come, Nanny, because I am – in terrible trouble!"

"Now how can you be in anything like that?" Nanny asked. "Sit down and let me look at you."

Odela sat down as she had been told and then pulled off her riding hat.

"You're as lovely as your mother!" Nanny exclaimed, "and I can't say fairer than that."

"Unfortunately it's not what I look like – but what I possess," Odela told her. "Oh, Nanny, you have – to help me."

"What's wrong?" Nanny asked, "I thought perhaps you'd find it difficult comin' back with her Ladyship there, but how have you got here so quickly?"

"I have – run away!"

"Alone?" Nanny asked in a horrified voice.

"No. I have brought Gatesy with me. She was the only person I knew in the whole house who I could ask – to accompany me."

She paused a moment and then added firmly,

"Now I have come here to you, I am not going back."

"What are you sayin'?" Nanny enquired rather nervously.

"I am saying, Nanny, that I have to stay here with you, at least until they find me. Then I will have to run away – somewhere else!"

Nanny sat down at the table again.

"What is all this about?" she asked, looking puzzled, "and what I've heard so far I don't like!"

"I know, Nanny, but you don't understand – what has happened to me."

Nanny's lips tightened.

"It's her Ladyship, I suppose!"

"Yes, it's her Ladyship," Odela agreed. "She has decided because Mama has left me a great deal of money that I am to marry the Viscount More!"

Nanny stared at her.

"I don't believe it!" she exclaimed.

"It's true, Nanny. I overheard them planning it through the communicating door when I was in Papa's bedroom and you know what Stepmama is like once she makes up her mind about something."

"I do indeed," Nanny muttered almost beneath her breath.

"So I knew I had to come – to you. You are the only person who can help me and if I stayed in London I would be married almost before I realised what was happening."

"So havin' heard what her Ladyship was plannin'," Nanny said as if she was trying to make the story clear in her own mind, "you ran away."

"I left with Gatesy yesterday morning and caught the six-thirty train to Oxford. I stayed last night at home and persuaded Robinson to bring me here to – you. He has sworn he will tell no one – where I am."

"You can trust Mr. Robinson," Nanny nodded.

"Yes, I know, and he has all my clothes in the horses' saddlebags."

"Well, we'd better get them upstairs at any rate," Nanny said, "and is that all?"

"I told Robinson that, when he was stabling Dragonfly, he was to say that I was a relative of yours – a 'Miss West'."

"If, lookin' as you do, people believe that," Nanny pronounced with a snort, "they'll believe anythin'."

"They *have* to believe it!" Odela cried. "Oh, Nanny, you must help me. How can I marry a man – who is in love with my stepmother?"

Nanny did not speak and Odela knew that she was aware of the relationship between her stepmother and the Viscount.

"You never mentioned anything about it in your letters," she said accusingly.

"It's not proper for you to know of such things," Nanny countered severely, "and it's a rank insult to your dear mother's memory."

"Of course it is," Odela agreed, "but I could not tell Papa, could I?"

"I should hope not, dearie, and it's somethin' you should not know about either."

"I overheard Stepmama telling the Viscount that once we were married he would control my fortune and Papa – because he and the Viscount's father are friends, would not think of him as a fortune-hunter."

"What fortune?" Nanny asked.

Odela realised that that gossip at any rate had not yet reached Coombe Court.

She told Nanny what her mother had left her and how she intended to do all the things that her mother had always wanted.

That was unless the husband she married prevented her from doing so.

"Why should I marry anyone?" Odela asked Nanny, "especially a man – who is in love with Stepmama."

"In love indeed!" Nanny squawked. "That's not love and don't you think of it like that."

Odela looked at her and she went on,

"Love's what your dear mother had for your father and comes from God Himself."

She snorted before she added,

"Anything that comes from that woman is the work of the Devil!"

Odela had never heard Nanny speak so fiercely or so fervently.

Then she said,

"You are right, Nanny, and I just knew that there was something wrong as soon as I entered the house, but I think in her own way, as long as he never finds her out, she makes Papa happy."

Nanny snorted again, but she did not speak and Odela said in a low voice,

"I think you – ought to have warned me,"

"I thought of it," Nanny admitted, "but it wasn't my business and naturally I had no idea that it would become yours."

"But it *is* mine," Odela said, "and please, Nanny, let me stay – with you."

"You can stay, of course, you can stay," Nanny agreed, "but for how long? You can't spend the rest of your life here and anyway it wouldn't be right."

"What do you mean by – that?" Odela asked her.

"His Lordship's a bachelor," Nanny replied, "and, if it was known that you were under his roof without a chaperone, you could get a bad name. And that's somethin' that your mother would never have approved of!"

"But – where can I go, Nanny?"

Odela suddenly felt like a child asking questions that only Nanny would know the answer for.

"We'll have to think about it," Nanny replied briskly. "But you can stay for the moment, because his Lordship's away and, if the rest of the staff are told you're a relative of mine, there should be no difficulties."

She paused before she added,

"Not that I can't see at least a hundred problems loomin' up in the future!"

Odela laughed because it was so like Nanny.

"Nothing matters," she said, "except that I can be with you, Nanny. It was what I wanted – all the time I was away."

Nanny's eyes softened.

"I've missed you too, dearie, more than I can say, but I'm comfortable enough here and little Betty's as good as gold."

As she spoke, she bent down and picked up the little girl in her arms.

"Aren't you, my pet?" she asked.

Odela could see Betty was a pretty child, but she looked very fragile.

As if she had asked the question, Nanny remarked,

"She wasn't strong enough for her Ladyship to take along when they were travellin' from one place to another."

She smiled at the child as she went on,

"His Lordship's on a special mission to India, Singapore and Heaven knows how many other places. They'll be away for nearly a year."

"Well, Betty is very lucky to have you, Nanny."

"That's what her Ladyship said and she remembered your mother and you when you were a little girl."

"I cannot remember her," Odela admitted.

"Why should you?" Nanny asked. "She was married when you were very small and her first husband was killed out huntin'."

"She had no children?" Odela asked.

"Not until she married for the second time," Nanny answered, "then she had Betty and she's hopin' her next one will be a son."

There was a little silence before Odela asked,

"If I marry, Nanny, or even if I was – living at home – you promised to come to me?"

"If you marry, I wouldn't go anywhere else," Nanny responded, "not if they offered me a million pounds! But I'll not go to any house where her Ladyship is, not after the way she turned me out as if I was dirt beneath her feet."

There was so much indignation in Nanny's voice that instinctively Odela stood up and put her arms around her.

"What we both have to do," she said, "is to keep out of sight of her Ladyship. You do understand, Nanny, that I cannot go back and – find myself in her clutches?"

"Of course you can't, dearie," Nanny agreed, "and it's over my dead body she'll marry you to that 'fancy man' of hers!"

Odela kissed her cheek.

"That is all I wanted you to say, Nanny, and now I am no longer frightened – so can we please send to the stables for my clothes?"

She reached out as she spoke and took Betty from Nanny's arms.

"I will look after Betty," she said, "and I will tell her that she is the luckiest little girl in the world because she has you as her Nanny."

"Now get along with you," Nanny replied, "and let me make it quite clear, I don't approve of what you're doin'. At the same time I can't for the life of me think what else you can do."

Odela laughed.

"Oh, Nanny, I love you. Now I know I am really home and back in the nursery!"

CHAPTER FOUR

Riding back to Coombe Court, Odela thought that she had spent the happiest few days she could ever remember.

It was so wonderful to be with Nanny again and to be able to read new and unusual books, but most of all to be able to ride Dragonfly.

Never had she imagined that any library could be as marvellous as the one she had found at Coombe Court. What made it even better was that the Curator had gone away on holiday.

There was therefore no one to interfere as she browsed among the bookshelves.

There had been a library at the Convent School in Florence and her father had a library at home, but the one at Coombe Court was different.

To begin with it had been built and filled with books at the same time as the house by the first Marquis of Trancombe.

A portrait of him hung over the mantelpiece and every successive Marquis had added to the library as well as all the house's fabulous treasures.

There were not only history books but those written by the authors of the time, politicians, Statesmen, engineers and finally novelists.

All the Waverley novels by Sir Walter Scott were there for her to read and enjoyed.

She could also, if she wished, read a first edition of *The Canterbury Tales*.

As soon as she had finished tea in the nursery and Nanny was getting Betty ready for her bath, Odela would go down to the library.

Whenever she went there, she felt that she must thank the Marquis who had built it.

She would stand in front of the mantelpiece looking up at his portrait and telling him how clever he had been.

It was actually a very handsome and intriguing face that she looked at.

He had been painted by Sir Anthony Van Dyck and Odela calculated because her father had told her about the famous painter that it must have been on his first visit to England in 1621 during the reign of King James I.

When he had come to England for the second time he had painted wonderful portraits of King Charles I besides a great number of the most famous people of the country.

Whichever visit it had been, he had certainly painted a remarkable and very striking portrait of the first Marquis of Trancombe.

He had outstanding features and was, Odela thought, the most handsome man she had ever seen.

The portrait was only a small one ending at the waist, but it showed the Marquis's long fingers and sensitive hands.

Hands exquisitely formed were a characteristic of Van Dyck and, of course, to Odela the Marquis's hands were exceptional.

'How could you have thought of anything so magnificent as this library?' Odela asked him silently.

She imagined that there was a twinkle in his eyes because he enjoyed her enthusiasm.

Now as she rode Dragonfly over the flat fields towards the stables, she told herself that she had been extremely lucky.

It would be difficult for her stepmother, if she was in fact looking for her, ever to be able to find her.

"I've told a lot of lies on your behalf," Nanny commented tartly, "and I'll doubtless suffer for them in the next world."

"What have you — said?" Odela asked her nervously.

"I told them downstairs you're my niece," Nanny replied, "and that my brother has a livery stable near Oxford. I had to account somehow for that horse of yours."

Odela had given a cry.

"Nanny, how clever of you!" she exclaimed. "I had forgotten that they would think Dragonfly looked too well bred and therefore — too expensive for a young woman to own."

"One lie leads to another," Nanny remarked, "and I only hopes if we're caught out, I'm not sent packin' without a reference!"

Odela laughed and put her arms round her.

"If you are 'sent packing' as you call it – you will come to me. And as far as I am concerned, Nanny, you can have my whole fortune and live like a Queen."

"That's the last thing I want to do," Nanny said sharply.

At the same time Odela knew that she was pleased at what she had just said.

There was the soft expression in Nanny's eyes that she had known ever since she was a baby.

'If only I could stay here for ever,' she thought now as she neared the beautiful house and thought that it opened its arms to welcome her.

She dismounted in the yard and put Dragonfly into his stall.

One of the stable lads hurriedly appeared when she had already taken off his saddle.

"I'll 'ang it up, Miss West," he said, taking the saddle from her, "but there be a real flapdoodle goin' on as 'is Lordship's just arrived."

Odela was suddenly still.

"His – Lordship?" she repeated.

"Aye, 'e just come with a party and never a word of warnin'."

He turned away to hang up the saddle.

Odela went rapidly from the stable into the house by the kitchen door and then ran up the stairs.

She burst into the nursery and, as Nanny looked up, she exclaimed,

"I hear the Marquis – has arrived."

"So I believe," Nanny replied quietly. "Now sit down and have your tea and don't fuss yourself. He won't be takin' any interest in you."

"I know that, but I don't want him – to see me."

"He'll not do that neither," Nanny answered, "as long as you behave yourself and stay up here."

Odela's heart sank.

She knew that it would prevent her from riding Dragonfly.

She also loved roaming around the house, as she had been doing for the last three or four days, when she had explored the marvellous salons, each called after different colours.

There was the Silver Salon, the Rose Salon and the Blue Salon.

As well there was a very charming sitting room, which was quite simply called 'the Cartoon Room'. In it were a number of amusing cartoons and political caricatures that had been collected by the family down the ages.

Some of them were so funny that they made her laugh out loud.

She enjoyed those by Hogarth and the very rude lampoons of the Prince Regent done by Rowlandson and Cruikshank.

There were so many things to see in Coombe Court that she thought it would take her weeks if not months before she had seen half of them.

Now, for as long as the Marquis was in residence, she must be confined to the nursery floor.

"Is it a – big party?" she asked Nanny aloud.

"I've no idea," Nanny replied, "and the less you bother your head about it the better."

Odela knew from the way she spoke that Nanny was a little nervous, although she would never have admitted it.

She realised that it would be a great mistake for the Marquis to learn of her existence and start asking awkward questions about her.

Odela finished her tea and played with Betty while Nanny made her bath ready.

She was a dear little girl, but very quiet and she was quite content to play by herself or with anybody else who could spare the time.

Odela built her a brick castle, which she enjoyed knocking down with a few giggles.

She then helped her to tidy away her dolls and the small pieces of furniture that belonged in the doll's house. Betty was then put to bed.

Odela was sitting in front of the fire opposite Nanny when an elderly housemaid came into the room.

"Have you got a bit of cotton you could let me have, Nanny?" she asked. "The lady I'm lookin' after has pulled a button off her gown and I forgot to get some from the carrier when he called."

"Yes, of course," Nanny said, rising to go to her sewing basket.

"His Lordship certainly picks 'em!" the housemaid remarked as she waited. "The last lady were pretty enough, but this one takes the cake, she does really."

Nanny who was searching in her sewing basket looked at Odela.

"I've put some handkerchiefs in your room for you to wash, dearie," she said, "and you'd better go and do so now before supper."

Odela smiled and she knew that Nanny disliked her hearing any gossip and that was why she was being sent away.

"Yes, of course, Auntie," she said aloud. "I will go them at once."

She thought when she reached her own bedroom that she would like to see the Marquis's choice.

She had certainly excited the admiration of the housemaid and then Odela told herself contemptuously that she was doubtless a married woman!

And like her stepmother she was being unfaithful to her husband.

The idea made her feel again the horror and shock it had been when she realised that her stepmother had a lover.

And also that she was determined that he should take over her fortune.

'There must be someone in the world who is decent, moral and respectable,' she thought frantically.

Then she told herself it was just the people who lived in London. They were part of the fashionable Society that her stepmother enjoyed so much.

Her mother had been perfectly content to live in the country and so Odela had never suspected anything like the depravity and immorality that went on in London.

'If that is what the Marquis enjoys,' she told herself, 'he does not deserve to have a beautiful house like this!'

When she returned to the nursery, the housemaid had left and, because she could not help being curious, she asked Nanny,

"Did you find out who was staying here?"

"There's the Earl and Countess of Avondale, who are quite elderly," Nanny replied, "and a Lady Beaton."

From the way Nanny spoke Odela guessed who it was who was embroiled with the Marquis.

"Now you forget them," Nanny went on, "and stay quiet here with me. If you want somethin' to occupy yourself, I'll give you some sewin' to do."

She gave a little snort before she went on,

"But I expect you'd rather stuff yourself with those books as you've brought upstairs."

Odela laughed.

"Of course I would! But I have promised you, Nanny, I will be no trouble, so don't worry about me."

"Of course I worry about you," Nanny replied. "You know that by this time your father and her Ladyship will be wonderin' when you'll be returnin' home."

"Then they will just have to wonder," Odela said quickly. "I am going to stay here with you and be *safe*."

Nanny duly went to bed early and, when Odela went to her own room, she felt once again that her stepmother was threatening her.

'I must forget her,' she told herself and climbing into bed, picked up her books.

It was then she realised that it was a book that she had already finished and she had also finished the other one that was lying beside the bed.

She had intended when she came in for tea to go to the library and change them, as she had done on other days.

If she had had any idea that the Marquis would be coming home, she would have picked out half-a-dozen or more books and brought them upstairs.

'I cannot go for days without reading,' she thought desperately.

She wished now that she had asked the housemaid how long the Marquis would be staying, but she thought that perhaps she did not know.

Thinking it over she knew that it was Friday and she suspected therefore that the Marquis and his party would stay until Monday.

That meant tonight, Saturday and Sunday, she would be confined to the nursery with nothing to read.

'I cannot bear it,' she thought.

She lay back against her pillows and told herself that the house party, if they had come from London, were not likely to stay up late.

Especially the Earl and Countess who were, as Nanny had told her, elderly.

'I will wait until everything is quiet,' Odela decided, 'then I will go down the backstairs to the library and collect as many books as I can carry.'

She felt that she would be perfectly safe and she knew from what she had seen of Coombe Court that the party would be likely to sit in the Blue Salon.

It was not as large as the Silver Salon and it was also near to the dining room, while the library was at the other end of the ground floor.

The Marquis would hardly be looking for books to read in the middle of the night, she ruminated.

No one was therefore likely to notice if she slipped down to choose some more for herself.

She picked up one of the books that she had already read, but found it impossible to concentrate on it.

Finally she jumped out of bed and walked over to the window to pull back the curtains.

The stars already filled the sky and there was a half-moon rising above the trees and it turned everything to silver.

The world seemed so beautiful she felt that she was being carried away on wings.

It was a Dreamland where she was loved by someone who would keep her safe and she would never be afraid again.

'If I could only find him,' she thought, 'we could live in a house like this and never go to London and never be involved with people like my stepmother.'

She felt as if her whole being was swept out into the moonlight.

She prayed that she could be part of its sublime beauty and that she would find the love that it personified.

'Please bring me love,' she prayed fervently, 'a love that is real and lasting. The love that men and women have sought since the very beginning of time.'

Then because it hurt her to think that such perfection could never be hers, she drew the curtains and went back to bed.

She must have fallen asleep and then she woke with a start to remember that she had wanted to go to the library.

She looked at the clock and saw that the hand pointed to the figure three and there would be nobody about at this time of the night.

Carefully she got out of bed and lit the candle in a candlestick that had a handle so that she could carry it.

She put on the pretty dressing gown that she had bought in Florence and the slippers that went with it. They made no sound as she walked slowly on tiptoe out onto the landing and down the stairs.

She found her way to the secondary staircase, which was at the far end of the next floor.

At the bottom of the stairs it was only a short walk down a darkened passage to the library.

Most of the candles in the passages had been extinguished, but there was just enough light for Odela to see her way.

But she would need her candle in the library, which was in complete darkness.

The great bookshelves seemed to tower above her to touch the painted ceiling.

She moved to the end of the library where she knew that there was some books that she particularly wanted to read.

As she went passed the mantelpiece, she lifted up her candle.

She looked at the handsome face of the first Marquis and thought that he smiled at her.

He would understand that it was impossible for her to be without books, which had obviously meant a great deal to him. Otherwise he would never have built the library.

Then she went on to the far end of the great room and she held her candle tightly so that she could see the titles clearly.

She began taking one book after another out of the shelves.

She had collected four that she particularly wanted and was looking for two more.

Then she heard a strange noise.

For a moment she could not think what it was.

It came again and she knew that it was the sound of breaking glass.

She stood still, wondering what was happening.

Suddenly she realised that somewhere at the other end of the library a window had been opened.

Although it seemed incredible, somebody was entering the room by one of the long diamond-paned casements that were ornamented on the top with the Coat of Arms of the Coombe family in stained glass.

Odela's first impulse was to go to see what was happening and then she remembered that she must not be found in the library and started to look for a hiding place.

Just beside her was a window with curtains drawn over it

Quickly she blew out the candle and slipped between the curtains, which were of heavy crimson velvet.

She found herself in the moonlight and it was streaming in through exactly the same sort of casement as she had heard being opened at the other end of the library.

Outside the stars were shining and the moonlight was illuminating the shrubs, the lawns and the endless flowerbeds.

Step by step she moved on tiptoe to the edge of the curtains that covered part of the wall beside the window.

Moving the curtain slightly so that it would not reveal the moonlight, she peeped through it.

The library should have been in complete darkness, but instead she could see that there was a man coming from behind one of the bookcases that hid the window that he must have entered through.

He was carrying a large lantern in his hand and holding it up so that he could see where he was going. It also illuminated his face.

Odela felt her heart give a start as she was aware that he was wearing a dark scarf reaching over his nose.

There was no doubt that he was a burglar.

She wondered frantically what she should do about it.

It seemed strange when there were so many treasures in the other part of the mansion that he should come to the library.

It flashed through her mind that he might be a connoisseur of books. In which case he would be searching for a first folio of Shakespeare or perhaps *The Canterbury Tales*.

This she had seen in one of the shelves and knew that it was very valuable.

Then, as he advanced down the library, she realised with horror that he was staring up at the portrait above the mantelpiece.

Could he really be intending to steal the Van Dyck portrait of the first Marquis?

She could not believe it was true.

He put the lantern down on the mantelpiece and she was aware that it was indeed what he intended.

Of course it was worth a great deal! All Van Dyck's portraits were.

Her father had often told her how much he wished that he possessed one.

'That man must not steal the portrait from Coombe Court,' Odela said to herself.

She could see that now both his hands were free and he was striving to lift the picture off the wall.

It was obviously more securely held to the wall than he had expected and he was pushing it upwards and trying to pull it off its hook.

Impatiently he removed the scarf from his face and flung it down on the floor. He also took off his hat and coat, dropping them beside it.

Then, as he turned back to look with determination at the portrait, the light was on his face.

With the greatest difficulty Odela stifled the cry that came to her lips.

She recognised the man!

In fact she knew him by sight and all about him.

He was a youngish man, under thirty, by the name of Fred Cotter.

His mother, who was a widow, lived in a small house which was a few miles from Shalford Hall.

Fred Cotter, Odela remembered, had been a problem for his family ever since she could remember.

She had heard her mother talking about him and saying how sorry she was for his parents and his father had been a Solicitor who was continually paying out money he could hardly afford in fines incurred by his son.

Fred Cotter had several times been wanted by the Police for theft of one kind or another, but they had never been able to find the goods on him.

His face had been recognised at the place of his crimes, but the local Magistrates had inevitably dismissed the cases through lack of evidence.

"He is a bad lot!" Odela could remember her father saying on several occasions.

Her mother's answer had always been the same,

"It is poor Mrs. Cotter I am sorry for," she would say. "He is her only child and he is breaking her heart, but however badly he behaves she still loves him."

Now peeping from behind the curtain Odela wondered if she should confront Fred Cotter.

She was just about to do so when she remembered one instance and it must have been about five years ago.

Fred had knocked down a man who had discovered him in his house and he had injured him so badly that the man had been taken to hospital.

Afterwards he was unable to give coherent evidence against Fred.

So once again he had 'got away with it'.

There was nothing therefore that Odela could do but watch Fred Cotter lift the portrait down from the mantelpiece.

He propped it against a chair and then he put on his hat and coat again and wrapped the scarf around his neck.

Picking up the lantern he held it in his left hand while with the other he carried the portrait.

The frame was heavy, but he took it to the end of the room and disappeared behind a bookcase.

Odela did not move, but she could still see the flickering light of the lantern.

She could hear a faint sound as Fred Cotter pushed the picture through the window and she had the idea that there was someone outside who was helping him, but she was not that sure.

She was only aware that the light of the lantern vanished and the window was pulled to.

Then there was silence.

She made no movement until she was certain that Fred Cotter had gone away and then it was safe for her to come from her hiding place.

As she did so, she pulled back the curtain so that the moonlight seeped into the library and she was able to see her way.

She could see the empty place over the mantelpiece where the portrait of the first Marquis of Trancombe had hung.

She looked up at it and knew that of all the pictures in Coombe Court this was the one that should not have been stolen.

It was the heart of the whole building. How then could it be lost to a horrible petty thief like Fred Cotter?

She tried to remember what he had stolen in the past and recalled that they were all antiques of some sort.

This meant, she thought, that he was in touch with a crooked dealer, who would pay without asking any questions for anything that was brought to him.

It was with a feeling of horror that she realised that the first Marquis's portrait might be sent abroad and never to be found again.

'I must stop him!' she told herself urgently.

Then she knew that the only person who could do that was the Marquis.

She stood still trying to think clearly.

The moonlight shining through the long high window made the library in its silver light as beautiful as the garden.

Yet there was that *empty* place over the mantelpiece.

Unless she did something about it, Odela thought, the library would never be the same again.

Fred with his greedy fingers had stolen the heart of Coombe Court.

"What shall I do? Oh, God, *what shall I do*?" she asked frantically.

To go direct to the Marquis and tell him what had happened would be to betray herself.

Perhaps if Fred was caught she would have to give evidence, first to the Police and then to the Magistrates.

How could she say that she was Nanny's niece?

Certainly she could not lie if she had to take an oath on the Bible.

'Help me – Mama – *help me*!' she prayed desperately.

Then, as if her mother answered her, she knew what she must do.

At the end of the library near to the window that Fred Cotter had entered through there was a desk.

It was where the Curator sat making notes of the new editions and checking those that were already in the shelves.

Just as Odela had pulled back the curtains from one window, Fred had moved the curtains from the one that he had entered through.

She pulled them back further and the light was as bright as any candelabrum.

She seated herself at the desk.

As she might have expected there was some writing paper engraved with the Marquis's crest in a leather folder.

She laid a piece of paper on the blotter and took up one of the white quill pens.

The inkpot, which apparently had been of no interest to Fred Cotter, was of gold.

Carefully thinking out every word, she wrote,

"The portrait of the first Marquis of Trancombe by Sir Anthony Van Dyck has been stolen by Fred Cotter of the Gable Cottage, Wichingham.

Having finished writing, she waited for the ink to dry.

As she looked down, she saw that pieces of broken glass were strewn all over the floor.

As soon as the housemaids came in first thing in the morning to clean the room, they would realise what had happened.

Then she was afraid that as the Curator was away they might not see the letter that she had written on the desk.

She knew, however, where it would be found.

Picking up her candle and carrying the letter in her hand, she walked to the door.

She opened it cautiously just in case anyone was about, but there were only long empty passages with candles burning in every other sconce.

She lit her own candle from one of them and made her way to the study.

She was sure that, like her father, the Marquis's secretary would place his letters on the desk each day.

Nanny had told her that there was no secretary at Coombe Court when she had arrived.

"Mr. Renolds is in London with his Lordship," she said, "and a good thing too."

"Why?" Odela enquired.

"Because I'd have had to ask his permission for you to stay here with me," Nanny replied. "As it is I had to ask no one and when Mr. Renolds does return it'll be too late for him to say anythin'."

Odela suspected, however, that Mr. Renolds would come back with his Master.

'The Marquis will see this first thing,' she assured herself, 'and with any luck they will catch Fred Cotter before he takes the painting to London or wherever he will try to sell it.'

She had looked at the study when she had been inspecting the house and, entering the room, she placed the letter she had written down on the blotter and no one who went to the desk could fail to see it.

It was only then that she remembered the books that she had selected in the library.

The servants would think it strange that Fred Cotter, before he removed the picture, had taken them from the shelves.

Quickly she hurried back and, before she picked up the four books that she had chosen, she pulled the curtains back into place.

Then she climbed up the stairs to her bedroom.

Only when she had closed the door behind her did she realise that her heart was beating frantically.

How could such a thing have happened?

How could she have been in the library and thus enable the Marquis to retrieve the precious portrait.

'There is no reason why anyone should suspect that I wrote the letter,' she told herself.

She climbed wearily into bed.

As she did so, she looked at the clock.

The hands now stood at four o'clock and it seemed incredible that so much had happened in just one hour.

As she blew out her candle, she thought to herself, 'No one will ever know it was me.'

*

The Marquis of Trancombe awoke.

For a moment he did not know where he was.

Then, as he realised that Elaine Beaton was sleeping peacefully beside him, he realised that they had both fallen asleep.

It was not surprising as their lovemaking had been fiery, exotic and inevitably exhausting.

The Marquis reckoned that it would soon be dawn and he must return to his own bedroom.

Very gently with the litheness of a man who had complete control over his athletic body, he slipped out of the bed.

Picking up a long robe that lay on a chair, he put it on and silently crossed the room.

Reaching the door he looked back, but Elaine had not moved.

He let himself out into the passage and was instantly aware of the difference in the air. He had found Elaine's French perfume overpowering and felt that he could breathe far better without it.

He walked towards his own room, but as he did so had a sudden desire for some fresh air.

He hesitated.

Then with a slightly mocking twist to his lips he moved further along the passage to where there was an oval-topped oak door.

He pulled back the bolt and opened it.

Inside there were some narrow steps that led, as the Marquis knew, up to the roof.

He had not climbed them for many years but it had been an activity that he had greatly enjoyed as a boy.

Now, as he felt a greater need for fresh air, he thought that it was like stepping back in time to use them again.

They were very steep and narrow and had been added to the house soon after it was built.

The Marquis pushed open the door at the top of the steps and it fell back with a bang onto the flat roof.

Then, as he climbed out on to the roof, he realised that he was at exactly the right moment.

The stars overhead were already receding and in the East there was the first faint light of the dawn. It was not cold and there was no wind.

As the Marquis stood up on the roof looking at the first ray of sunshine, that he was filled with the same joy he had known as a boy.

It was then that a new day had meant to him another step in the adventure of life. He moved forward into manhood when there were so many things for him to do and so much to be achieved.

Everything had been so full of promise and yet he had to admit that in some ways he was disappointed.

There was no reason why he should be, but he felt as if the world that he had seen from the top of his house had not turned out to be quite as exciting as he had expected it would be.

And he had not lived up to his own ideals.

'Perhaps I have not tried hard enough,' he reflected, 'or it is because I have lingered by the wayside picking flowers that inevitably die as soon as I possess them.'

He thought cynically that was what he already felt about Elaine Beaton.

She was a flower that he had desired and a flower that had seemed to him perfection until he made it his.

Then, like every other blossom, its petals had withered and he was ready to throw it away.

'How can I be so absurd?' he asked himself.

The first rays of the sun swept upwards from the distant horizon.

It was so incredibly beautiful as it seared its way through the last remnants of the night that he drew in his breath.

As he did so, he was aware of a movement below him and his eyes moved to the fields a little to his right.

For the moment he had been the only human being in a magic world, but there was now another.

A horse was coming in the direction of the stables and he was aware that it was being ridden by a woman.

He could not see her clearly but he was aware as she galloped away across the flat land that she rode extremely well.

Because from the top of the house he could see for a great distance he watched her move from one field to another.

She jumped two hedges with an expertise that was unmistakable and then finally, still riding very fast, she disappeared among the trees into what was known as 'Cliff Wood'.

'Now who can she be?' the Marquis asked himself.

Then the sun was in his eyes so that he could see no more.

He turned round and went down the steps back into the house.

CHAPTER FIVE

Odela had tried to sleep, but it was impossible.

Her heart was still thumping and she was dreadfully worried that Fred Cotter would dispose of the picture before anybody could stop him.

Supposing the Marquis, when he read her note, asked everybody in the house who had written it?

He would then discover that he had a guest in his house who he had never heard of and undoubtedly he would then demand to see her immediately.

'I must go away,' she decided, 'at least for the day.'

She jumped out of bed, dressed herself rapidly and ran to Nanny's room.

Nanny was fast asleep with Betty in her cot beside her.

Odela touched her shoulder and Nanny was instantly alert, as if one of her charges had called for her.

"It's me, Nanny," Odela whispered.

"What is it?" Nanny asked.

In a very low voice Odela recounted all that had happened.

"I remember that Fred Cotter," Nanny remarked. "He's a real bad one, he be!"

"Yes, I know, Nanny, and I could not let him take the beautiful Van Dyck portrait of the first Marquis."

She realised that Nanny had never seen it, but felt that she understood.

"I am going to take Dragonfly," Odela went on, "and stay out all day. By the time I return the Marquis will have his picture back and not be asking any more questions of the household."

Nanny seemed to think that this was the only thing to do.

Odela kissed her and tiptoed from the bedroom so that she should not waken Betty.

She ran down the stairs and going out through the back door saw that it was nearly dawn and that the stars were growing fainter overhead.

She went straight to Dragonfly's stall, which was at the far end of the stables. Everything was very quiet and she thought that the stable boy who was in charge was asleep.

It was no trouble for her to bridle and saddle Dragonfly as she had done it so many times before.

She led him out into the yard and stood him by the mounting block. He stayed still until she was safely seated in the saddle.

Then, as she picked up the reins, he moved, impatient to be off and delighted to be going out.

She took him out of the stables by the back way and onto the flat land.

Then she gave Dragonfly his head and settled down to really enjoy herself.

The Marquis was woken at eight o'clock by his valet pulling back the curtains.

He stretched out his arms still feeling tired after so few hours of sleep.

Then to his surprise his valet came to the side of the bed.

"Excuse me, my Lord," he said, "but Mr. Newton wants to see you urgent-like."

Newton was the butler and the Earl asked in surprise,

"What does he want?"

"'E'll tell you 'imself, my Lord," the valet replied and went to open the door.

The Marquis raised himself on his pillows and pushed the hair back from his forehead.

As the butler came into the room, he asked sharply,

"What is this all about, Newton?"

"I'm sorry to disturb your Lordship," Newton replied, "but someone's broken into the house and the picture over the mantelshelf in the library has been stolen!"

If he had intended to astonish the Marquis, he certainly succeeded.

The Marquis stared at him before he exclaimed,

"I don't believe it! Where was the nightwatchman?"

"I'm afraid, your Lordship, we're without one at the moment. Clements was taken ill and we've been expecting him back any day, but he has not yet recovered."

"Why was I not told about this?" the Marquis demanded angrily.

"The burglar broke in through the window, my Lord," Newton went on, "and there's glass all over the floor."

"I will come to see for myself," the Marquis replied.

He climbed out of bed and Newton hurried from the room.

The Marquis started to dress quickly, thinking furiously that it was sheer incompetence that this should have happened.

It was always the same, he thought, if he was away for any length of time. The staff grew lax and anyway Clements was getting too old to be a nightwatchman.

He told himself that he should have thought of engaging a second man a long time ago.

In the meantime, if he lost the portrait of the first Marquis by Van Dyck, it was irreplaceable.

It was a painting that his father had always been extremely proud of and he had had it cleaned and reframed just before his death.

The Marquis could remember when he was a small boy being told that Van Dyck was a genius and there had never been a portrait painter to equal him anywhere in the world.

'How can I possibly lose anything so precious?' he asked himself furiously.

He was shaving himself when there was a knock on the door.

When his valet went to open it, he could hear somebody speaking to him in an urgent tone.

A moment later Mr. Renolds, his secretary, came rushing into the bedroom.

"I was just on my way down to find out what has occurred," the Marquis said in an irritated tone.

"What I have brought you, my Lord," Mr. Renolds stated rather breathlessly, coming nearer to him, "is this!"

He held out the note that Odela had left on the desk in the study.

The Marquis put down his razor and took it from him.

When he read it, he did not speak, but read it again to make quite sure that he was not mistaken.

"Where did you find this?" he asked.

"It was on the blotter in your study, my Lord."

"Who has written it?"

"I have no idea, my Lord."

The Marquis realised at once that the handwriting, which was very elegant, belonged to someone well-educated.

"It must have been somebody in the house," he declared.

"It's not the writing of any of the staff," Mr. Renolds answered.

The Marquis put the note down on his dressing table.

"If the information is correct," he said, "we had better hurry. Order Saracen to be round at the front door as quickly as possible and the two grooms, Ben and Dick, are to accompany me on horseback."

Without speaking Mr. Renolds started towards the door and the Marquis ordered,

"I shall want a pistol and they too had better be armed."

"I will see to it, my Lord."

Mr. Renolds's voice came back to him as he was running down the passage.

The Marquis was helped into his riding boots by his valet and he put on his whipcord riding coat.

Then he picked up Odela's note from the dressing table and hurried down the stairs.

"Breakfast is ready, my Lord," Newton announced.

But the Marquis walked past him and out through the front door.

The horses were already coming from the stables and he saw that the two grooms were hefty young men and he knew that they would prove their strength if they were involved in a fight.

The Marquis flung himself into the saddle and rode off at a swift pace.

He knew the way to Wichingham and it was far quicker across the fields than on the highway.

Saracen was fresh and skittish and, by the time the Marquis had to take to the road to enter the village, he was obliged to wait for some minutes for the two grooms to catch up with him.

As they rode on, he spoke for the first time.

"Your pistols are loaded?"

"Aye, my Lord."

"You are not to use them except as a very last resort. With any luck we will take the man by surprise so there should be no need for anybody to be injured."

He saw that the two grooms understood and only as the Marquis reached the first cottage in the village did he say to Ben,

"Do you know which is Gable Cottage?"

He was quite sure before he came downstairs that everybody in the house and in the stables would know about what was written on the note in his study.

Ben nodded.

"Aye, my Lord. 'Tis the first 'ouse beyond the Church."

The Marquis rode on.

The people he passed recognised him and the women dropped a curtsey while the men touched their forelocks.

Gable Cottage was larger than the other small thatched blue and white cottages. It was in fact more of a house with two large gables over the rooms on the first floor.

The garden was bright with spring flowers and the paved path that led up to the front door was neat and weeded.

A brass knocker on the door had been polished and there was a small garden at the back of the house and beyond it an open field.

The Marquis turned to Dick and said in a low voice,

"Ride round to the back of the house and let no one escape."

The groom did as he was told and the Marquis ordered Ben,

"You, watch the front."

He dismounted and tied Saracen to a post on the side of the gate.

Then he walked up the flagged path and turned the handle of the front door.

He thought that it was unlikely to be locked at this time of the day and he was not mistaken.

He walked into a small hall with some narrow stairs on one side of it leading up to the bedrooms.

There were two doors for him to could choose from and he took the furthest thinking that it would look out over the garden at the back.

Whoever occupied it would not have seen them arrive.

He opened the door and his instinct had been correct.

Sitting at a table in the centre of the room was a young man inspecting the Van Dyck portrait that lay in front of him.

He jumped to his feet as the Marquis appeared and was obviously startled and afraid.

The Marquis thought that he was an unpleasant-looking young man with a crafty look about him, which would have warned anybody who was observant that he was not to be trusted.

The Marquis walked to the table and put his hand on the picture frame.

"How dare you break into my house and steal my property!" he asserted. "I intend to take you to the Police Station and you will appear before the Magistrates. I expect you know the penalty for stealing?"

Fred Cotter did not answer, but the Marquis thought that his teeth were chattering.

"It is to be hanged," he went on, "or else transported. Is this your first offence?"

It was then that Fred Cotter went down on his knees.

"Forgive me, my Lord, forgive me," he pleaded with tears in his eyes. "My mother's ill and I'd no money to pay the doctor or for the medicine he ordered for her. I was tryin' to save her life!"

"You must have been aware that to steal a picture from my house would mean that the Police would be looking for the culprit and that you had little chance of getting away?"

"I know, I know!" Fred Cotter sobbed, "but I couldn't think how else to save my mother."

"I suppose you are aware that it would be unlikely that you could sell a picture of such high value and so easily identifiable?" the Marquis said scornfully.

"I didn't know that and it's the first time I've ever done such a thing, all I could think of was that I must save my mother."

Ten minutes later the Marquis left Gable Cottage with the portrait.

A weeping Fred Cotter had kissed his boots for saying that he would not be prosecuted.

"If you ever do such a thing again," the Marquis said warningly, "I shall not hesitate to see that you get your just deserts."

He gave the burglar a hard look before he went on,

"You can tell the doctor to send his bills to me for the medicines your mother requires and don't tell her how nearly she lost her son for good!"

"I promise, I promise!" Fred Cotter cried.

The Marquis walked out of the cottage handing the picture to Dick, who had to hold it on the front of his saddle with both hands.

The Marquis therefore told Ben to lead his horse and for both of them to ride slowly back to Coombe Court.

They took the smooth but long way by the highway and up the drive.

The Marquis rode back across the fields.

He had not only been merciful to Fred Cotter because of his pitiful tale about his mother and he had also thought that it was a mistake for the neighbourhood to know how easy it had been to break into Coombe Court without anybody being aware of it.

There were so many treasures in the different rooms.

There was a fine collection of snuffboxes, many of them decorated with diamonds and other precious stones.

There was copious porcelain with a priceless collection of *Sèvres* and *Dresden* china.

There was also his father's unique collection of ancient guns and pictures on every wall to delight the connoisseur.

'I will put two nightwatchmen on duty immediately,' the Marquis told himself, 'and this situation will most definitely not arise again.'

He reached the house to find that Newton and Mr. Renolds were waiting for him in the hall.

"I have my picture back," the Marquis announced, "but I blame both of you for your negligence in not seeing that the house was properly patrolled at night."

His voice was stern as he carried on,

"From now on there will be two nightwatchmen moving round the building all night. The catches on the windows and doors on the ground floor are to be reinforced so that it is impossible for anyone breaking the glass to gain access."

He spoke sharply and then walked into the breakfast room.

Neither of the men he was speaking to made any reply.

He ate an excellent breakfast and was joined by Lord Avondale and he said nothing to him of what had occurred last night.

It was then that he began to wonder once again who had given him the information that had enabled him to retrieve the precious portrait.

He went to his study and, when Mr. Renolds joined him, he asked,

"Have you discovered who wrote the note, Renolds? The least I can do is to thank my informant."

"I have no idea who it could have been, my Lord," Mr. Renolds replied.

Then he hesitated and the Marquis enquired,

"What is it?"

"Well, I know it seems unlikely to be the person we are seeking, but her Ladyship's Nanny has her niece staying with her."

"Her niece?" the Marquis repeated as if to himself. "Well, if you are quite certain none of the servants in the house wrote the note, I had better see this young woman. What is her name?"

"I have already ascertained, my Lord, that her name is West. Odela West."

"Then send for her," the Marquis ordered. "If she is my informant, I am definitely in her debt."

Mr. Renolds went from the room and it was some time before he returned.

Then, as the Marquis looked up at him expectantly, he said, "I am afraid, my Lord, Miss West has gone riding and no one seems to know when she will be back."

"Gone riding?" the Marquis repeated. "On one of my horses?"

"No, my Lord, on her own."

The Marquis looked surprised.

"Surely it is unusual for a woman in the position of nurserymaid to own a horse?"

"I understand, my Lord," Mr. Renolds replied, "that Nanny's brother has a livery stable in Oxford."

The Marquis smiled.

"Then that accounts for the horse. Leave a message to say that I would like to see her when she returns."

It was later in the day and Elaine Beaton had gone to rest, inviting him to join her, which he had no intention of doing.

The Marquis asked again for Odela West only to be informed that she had not yet returned.

It was then that he was aware, and he had not thought of it before, that she must have been the woman he had seen at dawn.

She had ridden from the stables towards Cliff Wood and it struck him that it was a strange thing to do so early in the morning and still stranger that she had not come back.

He was not only curious but he suddenly had an intuition that this was important.

He did not know the reason why, he just knew instinctively that this was something that he should investigate.

He glanced at the clock, it was two hours before he need dress for dinner.

He sent a message to the stables to say that he required Jupiter who was another of his favourite stallions.

Ten minutes later he was riding over the same flat fields where he had seen Odela in the morning.

Jupiter cleared the same hedges with ease and as he did so the Marquis was aware that they were too high for a woman.

Then he reached the wood.

Cliff Wood was the most attractive, and certainly the most beautiful wood on his whole Estate.

It had taken its name from the fact that the far end of it was on the side of a steep hill.

This was covered with shrubs but there was a cliff, which dropped down hundreds of feet into the valley below.

The view from the top was panoramic and also breathtakingly beautiful.

Anyone who came to stay at Coombe Court and enjoyed riding was always taken to see the view from Cliff Wood.

It was the Marquis's father who had put a wooden seat there and viewers could sit in comfort as they gazed in wonder at the panoramic view in front of them that extended for at least thirty miles.

The Marquis, following his instinct was sure for no reason, except that he 'felt it in his bones', as his Nanny would say, that this was where he would find the mysterious Odela West.

He was not mistaken.

*

Odela, having left Coombe Court precipitately so early in the morning had spent, although she had not expected to, a fascinating day.

First she had ridden Dragonfly very fast until they were both content to settle down to an easy trot.

Then, as she moved through the wood, she was enchanted as she always was.

The sun was flickering through the leaves of the trees, the birds were singing on the boughs and the rabbits were scuttling ahead of her.

She did not at first find her way to the lookout.

Instead she passed through the wood and going down the steep cliff, but at a lower angle and by a twisting path, she found herself in a small village.

She could not remember visiting it before.

It consisted only of an ancient black and white inn that was on a green with the traditional pond on which swam a mother duck with her newly hatched ducklings.

She saw to her delight some ancient stocks that had been used in Medieval times.

There were about half-a-dozen black and white thatched cottages surrounding the green.

By now, having had no breakfast, she was beginning to feel hungry.

She thought it was unlikely that anyone would recognise her and there seemed very few people about so she went to the inn.

There she asked the landlord if she could stable her horse while he gave her some breakfast.

"My groom is following me," she explained, "but my dog got lost in the wood and he is searching for him."

"I understand, ma'am," the innkeeper said, "and that there wood's an easy place to get lost in. We knows that in the village as the children play there."

Because it was a warm day Odela had her breakfast outside on a roughly hewn table made from the trunk of a tree and she suspected that it was where the old men sat in the evening drinking their ale and gossiping.

Because she was hungry the well cooked eggs and bacon tasted delicious.

She suspected that the coffee would not be of the best quality so instead she drank some strong tea, which she sweetened with a spoonful of honey.

The innkeeper's wife brought her a cottage loaf hot from the oven and she spread honey on it with golden butter, which came, she was told, from a nearby farm.

"This is a very pretty place," Odela remarked when she had finished eating.

"We likes to think so," the innkeeper said. "But we don't get many strangers round 'ere."

Odela thanked him, paid him the very little money he asked for the excellent breakfast and rode away on Dragonfly

She told him that she was going to meet her groom and help him to find her dog.

She rode a little further into a part of the country that she did not know.

Then she was concerned that she might meet somebody who had been to Shalford Hall who would recognise her.

She therefore rode up the hill and back into Cliff Wood.

It was then that she found the wooden seat.

There was no doubt why it had been put there and she sat entranced by what seemed like the world spread out beneath her.

First she knotted the reins round Dragonfly's neck and left him to wander where he wished.

She knew that he would not go far from her and she had only to call or whistle and he would come straight to her side. She had trained him since he was a foal and he was very obedient.

The day had passed slowly and yet she was happy without even a book to amuse her.

She loved the song of the birds in the wood and, as she always did when she was alone, she told herself Fairy stories.

She felt that she was living in them and they were as real to her as her own life.

It was only when the afternoon came that she began to feel very tired.

She had not slept all night and her agitation and horror at seeing Fred Cotter stealing the portrait of the first Marquis in the library had taken its toll.

She took off her riding hat and then her jacket, which she folded so that it made a pillow that she could rest her head on.

Then she lay down as she thought that she should relax.

She had no idea when she fell asleep.

*

The Marquis saw first Dragonfly, who was trying to find some blades of young grass where the trees ended.

He very much appreciated the superlatively well bred stallion, which he would have liked to own himself.

Then, as he looked at the wooden seat, he realised that his search was over.

But he had not expected to find Odela West lying fast asleep.

The sun, which was sinking low on the horizon, turned Odela's hair to gold and her eyelashes were dark against her cheeks.

The Marquis dismounted and knotted Jupiter's reins together and left him as free to roam as Dragonfly.

Then he walked to the wooden seat to look down at its sleeping occupant.

He was astonished and at the same time intrigued by what he saw.

How could anyone so beautiful in a very unique way be the nurserymaid who he was told had gone riding?

Everything about the sleeping girl proclaimed her to be as well bred as her horse.

Her oval forehead, her straight little nose and her long elegant neck. Her hands, one of which rested on her breast, might have been painted by Van Dyck himself.

As he stood gazing at her, the Marquis thought that she was most certainly a *Sleeping Beauty*.

He suddenly had an almost uncontrollable impulse to kiss her awake as in the Fairytale.

Then he told himself that it would be a most reprehensible thing to do to a girl who was related to one of the servants in his house.

Instead he coughed and the sound, as he had expected it would, awoke Odela.

Slowly she opened her eyes.

Then, as she looked at him, there was an almost incredulous expression in her eyes that he did not understand.

He had taken off his tall hat as he had approached the wooden seat.

He had no idea that to Odela he was the first Marquis come to life.

As he resembled so many of his predecessors, it had never for a moment occurred to the Marquis that he particularly looked like the first Marquis.

He was, as it happened, very like his father and also his great-grandfather, but there was indeed a strong family resemblance amongst them all.

But to Odela he personified exactly the portrait that she had gazed at every day.

The portrait that she had seen to her horror being stolen away by Fred Cotter.

For one moment they both stared at each other and then Odela said in a voice that did not sound like her own,

"Y-you – are alive! I-I thought you had – been – stolen."

Only as she spoke did she realise that she was awake and no longer dreaming and with an effort she sat up with her legs still on the seat.

Then the Marquis sat down in the space that was now available.

"I thought I would find you here," he began.

"How – how could you have – thought that?" Odela asked.

Then she gave a little cry.

"You have – saved the picture? Fred Cotter has not – disposed of it?"

"Thanks to you," the Marquis replied in his deep voice. "I discovered the portrait in Cotter's house and it is now back in its proper place in the library."

Odela gave a deep sigh of relief.

"I am so – glad."

"How could you have known, how could you have guessed that it was being stolen?" the Marquis quizzed her.

For a moment Odela hesitated.

Then she smiled and the Marquis thought that it was the most attractive thing that he had ever seen in his life.

"I had gone downstairs," she replied, "in the – middle of the night to – borrow some of your – books!"

The Marquis laughed.

"And so you disturbed Cotter?"

"No – he disturbed me," Odela replied. "I hid behind the curtain and, when I realised what he – was doing, I was – horrified!"

"I am extremely thankful that you were there at the right moment," the Marquis said. "At the same time why should you care?"

"Of course – I care. It would have been a dreadful tragedy to lose a painting that was so unique and – so important to Coombe Court."

She had a sudden thought.

"Suppose it had been – taken abroad? You would never have – seen it again."

"I am very grateful to you," the Marquis answered, "more grateful than I can possibly say and, of course, I am incredibly lucky that you were staying in my house."

He did not miss as he spoke, the colour that came into Odela's cheeks and that she looked away from him.

There was a silence between them until he said,

"I think I know why you are staying with me and why you ran away so early this morning. It was in case I should send for you."

"How do – you know I – did that?" Odela stammered.

"I happened to be up on the roof as the dawn broke and I saw you riding from the stables and taking those high hedges with a brilliance that I just could not help admiring."

"Dragonfly enjoys jumping them," Odela said simply.

"He is a magnificent animal!" the Marquis remarked as he looked towards where Dragonfly and Jupiter were close together.

"I have had him since he was a foal," Odela said. "I love him more than anything else in – the whole world."

There was a little throb in her voice that the Marquis thought was very moving.

After a moment's silence he commented,

"I think that, while today you were hiding from me, you are also hiding from somebody else."

What he said startled Odela.

She had been talking to him as she would have talked to any man she had met at home.

Now she remembered that she was in hiding and it was imperative that the Marquis should not be suspicious of her.

"I-I don't know – what you – mean," she stuttered.

"I think you do," the Marquis contradicted her. "But I don't want to upset you and I promise you that if it is possible, I will help you."

She looked at him wide-eyed.

"Why should you say – that?"

"As I have already told you, I am using my instinct and I think perhaps it is something that you do too."

"Yes – I do," Odela replied surprised that he should be aware of it.

"Then your instinct should tell you that you can trust me," the Marquis continued, "and I am going to risk your anger by saying that I don't believe for one moment that you are the niece of my sister's Nanny."

He paused a moment before resuming,

"Nor, as I have been told, that your father keeps a livery stable and Dragonfly is one of his horses."

Odela put up her hands as if to protect herself before she replied,

"You are – frightening – me. How can you – possibly know all – this?"

The Marquis smiled.

"I am not completely nitwitted! When I saw you asleep just now, I thought that you were *Sleeping Beauty*, the Princess who was woken only by a kiss!"

Odela blushed again.

Then she gave a little laugh.

"I was starting to tell myself a Fairy story when I fell asleep. Then when I woke and – saw you – "

" – And you thought that I was the first Marquis!" he finished.

"I-I must have been – dreaming of – him."

"I should be very flattered if you dreamed of me," the Marquis said.

There was a short silence and then Odela said hastily as if she wanted to change the subject.

"What have you done about – Fred Cotter?"

"Nothing," the Marquis replied.

"Nothing!" Odela exclaimed.

"He told me that his mother was very ill and he stole the portrait to pay for the medicines she needed."

He looked at her before he added,

"He wept very convincingly so, having given him a good lecture, I took back the painting and let him go free."

Odela sighed.

"That was very kind of you – but misguided. This man is a habitual thief. He is a disgrace to his family.

He spent all the money his father made and – I suspect all that his mother possesses."

The Marquis was looking at her with a startled expression as she went on,

"He has stolen dozens of times, but, as the goods have never been found, he has always been released – through lack of circumstantial evidence."

"I had no idea of that," the Marquis exclaimed, "but in any case, I thought it would be a mistake to have anything published about how easy it had been for him to break into my house."

Odela gave a little cry.

"You think other people might try to do the same thing? Oh, you must be careful! You must protect your glorious treasures."

"That is what I intend to do," the Marquis agreed, "and why two nightwatchmen will from now on always be on duty, so I think we should be safe enough in the future."

He saw the relief in Odela's eyes and his own twinkled as he said,

"Of course you will have to be careful when you are borrowing my books from the library or you may find yourself arrested!"

"Oh, please," Odela pleaded, "please allow me to go on – reading them. I have been so happy these last few days being able to ride Dragonfly, admiring your treasures and reading your books."

"And hoping that no one will discover where you are?" the Marquis pointed out.

"Why – do you say – that?"

"Because it is true, is it not?"

Odela gave up the struggle.

"It is true," she said, "but – please – please – don't ask any more questions and don't tell anybody, especially your guests that I am staying at Coombe Court."

"Are you afraid," the Marquis asked, working it out for himself, "that they might talk in London and that would let whoever was looking for you know where you are?"

"Stop! Stop. You are – too inquisitive – or too clever – I am – not sure which," Odela said accusingly.

"I am merely trying to help you."

"I can tell you how you can help me – and that is to forget me and go back now – and never think of me again."

The Marquis settled himself more comfortably on the wooden seat, resting his right arm along the top of it.

"You know that is impossible. How could you ask any man, especially one you think is clever, to forget that he has found that *Sleeping Beauty* is in his Castle and being foolish enough not to kiss her when he had the opportunity!"

"If you – talk to me – like that," Odela retorted, "Nanny – will be – very shocked!"

"I presume that she was your Nanny when you were a child," the Marquis remarked.

Odela gave a little scream.

"Go – away!" she cried. "You are – uncanny and, if you are – real and have not – stepped out of a picture, then you are – a wizard – and I don't – want to know you."

The Marquis laughed.

"Nonsense! You will enjoy knowing me as I shall enjoy knowing you and, if we have to meet secretly, we can always come here."

Odela did not answer and after a moment he went on,

"No on second thoughts this is too well known a beauty spot. I have a better idea."

"I am not – listening to you," Odela asserted. "Nanny brought me up – very strictly – and as I have no other – chaperone I have to do – what she tells me."

"If you tell Nanny this, I shall inform my guests of the exciting experience I have had," the Marquis warned.

"That is sheer blackmail," Odela accused him, "and you are worse than – Fred Cotter!"

"But much better looking!" the Marquis quipped.

Because she could not help herself Odela laughed.

The Marquis was thinking that he had never met anybody so attractive or for that matter so lovely and ethereal

She was so obviously different from any other woman he had ever known.

He was intrigued and excited in a way that he could not explain to himself.

He bent towards her.

"Now listen, Odela," he said, "because you wish to hide and I am delighted for you to do so in my house, you have to promise me, and it is only fair, that you will not hide from me."

"But – the servants – will know," Odela objected at once, "and, as you are – well aware, they – talk more than – anybody else."

"That is true," the Marquis said, "so it means we cannot meet inside the house, only outside."

"We should not meet – at all!"

"Think how disappointing it would be if, after this fascinating conversation, you ride away in one direction and I in another and we decide never to see each other again."

He spoke very beguilingly and Odela looked down shyly and her eyelashes swept her cheeks.

"It is – what we – ought to do," she said hesitatingly.

"How can you be so unadventurous or so dull?" the Marquis asked.

There was a little flash from her eyes and he knew that he had said the right words. No woman with any imagination would wish to be thought dull.

He seized his opportunity and then went on,

"What I am going to suggest is that I return in front of you so that no one will guess for one moment that we have met."

He paused and then went on,

"Tomorrow I am going to tell my guests that I have had an urgent request from the Queen to visit her at Windsor Castle."

Odela looked at him with startled eyes as he continued,

"No one will question that it is a duty that I must perform and I will therefore take my party back to London before luncheon."

"How can you do – that?" Odela asked.

"Very easily," the Marquis replied, "it is simply a question of organisation. When we have left, you will watch over the house until I return."

He smiled before he added,

"You may take all the books you wish from the library, but you will not have time to read many of them before I do return."

"And when – will that – be?"

She did not mean to encourage him by asking the question, it came to her lips before she could prevent it.

"On Sunday," he said, "and I will meet you after luncheon at the Folly. Do you know where that is?"

"I have seen it in the distance. It is beyond another wood you own that is as beautiful as this one."

"Not quite," the Marquis replied, "but the Folly is on the other side of it and I gave orders some years ago that no one was to go near it because it was unsafe."

"Unsafe?" Odela queried.

"Not now. I had it put in order and spent quite a lot of money on having it renovated inside.

"And no one goes – there?"

"I saw no reason to make it a place of assignation for the local lovers who would scribble their initials on the walls after I had had them repaired."

He smiled at her and then continued,

"Nor for the children who would light bonfires or fall off the top of it, which would mean I would have to pay for their broken bones!"

Odela laughed.

"I can see your reasons, but I think they are rather selfish."

"Not at all," the Marquis said defensively. "I am merely being cautious. Now I can meet you there and no one will have the slightest idea of what we are doing."

"I have not said – I will meet you," Odela protested.

"I cannot believe you would be so hard-hearted and indifferent to something that is exciting for us both."

"But – think how Nanny would – disapprove if she knew – about it," Odela retorted.

She knew as she spoke that she would be unable to resist the Marquis's plan.

And whatever difficulties there might be, she would ride to the Folly on Sunday.

CHAPTER SIX

Odela was amused when the servants kept coming into the nursery to tell Nanny how surprised they were that the Marquis was leaving so unexpectedly.

"It were hardly worth His Lordship comin'!" the Head Housemaid exclaimed, "and I can tell you Lady Beaton's in a real rage about it!"

When they had left, Odela went to the library.

She looked with delight at the first Marquis back in his rightful place over the mantelpiece.

Now she could see how extraordinary the likeness was between him and the Marquis.

'They are both very very handsome,' she thought.

It was an effort to leave the portrait and go to the bookshelves.

The locks on the casements had all been reinforced and she had learnt that there were now two stalwart nightwatchmen to patrol the house every hour of the night.

She thought happily that now she had met the Marquis she would be able to borrow his books, this time with his permission.

There would be no harm in creeping down to the library in the darkness again.

At the same time it was a very good thing that she had on that fateful night.

"I saved you," she said out loud triumphantly to the first Marquis before she left the library.

Although she chided herself for being ridiculous, she knew that she was counting the hours until Sunday.

'His Lordship will doubtless be delayed in London or decide that he has no wish to come back,' she tried to say to herself at one point.

But her instinct told her that he would keep his word.

And he would meet her at the Folly as they had planned.

*

On Sunday morning she went in to the nursery for breakfast with Nanny, who said,

"His Lordship came back very late last night and that means you'll have to stay up here and make sure he doesn't see you."

"I expect he will be busy, otherwise he would not have returned," Odela remarked. "But he will not see me if I go out through the back way – and you know how much I want to ride Dragonfly."

Nanny argued about it for a while.

Finally Odela had her own way after agreeing that she would go to Church with Nanny and Betty.

"I've ordered a carriage," Nanny told her, "and because she's a good little girl, Betty'll sit still and enjoy the singin', but we'll leave before the sermon."

There were not many people in the small village Church.

Odela prayed that she would not be discovered and that she could remain at Coombe Court with Nanny.

She felt sure that both God and her mother would hear her prayers.

When they drove back to the house, she felt so happy that she wanted to sing a psalm of praise all of her own.

She ignored the little voice inside herself that told her she was happy because she was going to see the Marquis.

'It's just – an adventure,' she told herself as she put on her riding habit, 'and doubtless he will return to London tomorrow – and never think of me again.'

She knew, however, that she would be thinking of him and it would be impossible to go into the library without doing so.

One of the young grooms saddled Dragonfly for her and she rode off, keeping out of sight of the house and so taking a longer route to the Folly.

She emerged from the wood beneath it.

It looked very impressive, silhouetted against the blue sky.

There was no sign of the Marquis or his horse and, as Dragonfly climbed up the hill to the Folly, Odela told herself that he had forgotten.

It was, of course, what she might have expected.

Then, as she dismounted, he was there, standing in the doorway of the Folly.

She felt her heart leap as he exclaimed,

"You have come! I was so afraid you might have forgotten."

"I thought you *had* forgotten," Odela said, "when I could not see your horse."

"I have hidden Saracen on the other side of the Folly," he told her, "and that is where I will put Dragonfly as well."

He took the bridle and led Dragonfly round the Folly while Odela went inside.

When she saw how attractive the interior was, she understood why the Marquis had no wish for visitors.

There was some beautiful plasterwork, mosaics and ornate windows. The floor was paved and in the centre was an ancient and attractively carved fountain and over it was a sculpted Cupid with a dolphin in his arms.

The fountain was not playing, but Odela reckoned that it had been created by a Master hand and was very valuable. There were several stone seats also with carved ends.

She sat down on one to wait for the Marquis. And without thinking she pulled off her riding hat.

She had no idea how lovely her fair hair looked against the ancient wall behind her.

The Marquis came in and, walking slowly towards her, said,

"I have loved the Folly ever since I was a child, but, when I restored it, I felt that there was something missing and now I know it was you."

"That is the nicest compliment I have ever had," Odela replied, "and I think your Folly is enchanting."

"That is what I think too," the Marquis nodded.

But he was looking at her and, instead of sitting beside her, he sat down on the edge of the fountain facing her.

"Now, tell me what has been happening while I have been away."

Odela laughed.

"Nothing, thank Goodness! I think we have had enough drama – to last us for a very long time!"

"Is that how long you are going to stay with me?" he enquired.

There was something in his voice that made Odela blush.

"Whatever – happens," she replied after a moment's pause, "I must not – impose on – you."

"You know perfectly well you are not imposing on me or anybody else," the Marquis said, "but I would like you to trust me with your secret."

Odela shook her head.

"It – would be a – mistake."

"Why?"

She thought for a moment before she answered him,

"For many reasons I don't want to talk about it – not here at any rate."

"You are quite right," the Marquis said, "but I suppose you know what I want to talk to you about in the Folly!

"What is – that?" Odela asked innocently.

He rose to his feet and taking her hand drew her to the end of the building where there was a carving on the wall that she had not noticed before.

It was very skilfully done and it was, she could see, of a man and woman gazing into each other's eyes and above them were three Cupids flying in the sky and holding up a garland of flowers.

"What do you think they are talking about?" the Marquis asked.

"I-I am – admiring the way it is – carved," Odela said hesitatingly.

"I am waiting for you to answer my question," he insisted.

She looked up at him and then quickly away again.

Her heart was beating faster and she suddenly felt breathless, as if it was impossible to speak.

It was then, at that moment, they heard a step behind them.

As Odela tried to turn round, someone grasped her arms and pulled them behind her back.

Equally she realised with horror that the same was being done to the Marquis by a huge man.

As she tried to struggle free, a voice piped up,

"I might have guessed, my Lady, it were you who recognised me and that's somethin' you're goin' to regret!"

It was Fred Cotter!

As Odela saw his crafty face, she felt the terror of it streak through her.

The Marquis was struggling and fighting as best he could, but the huge man had taken him at a disadvantage and was already winding a rope tightly round his body.

Odela felt Fred Cotter doing the same to her and the rope was crushing her breasts.

Almost before she could realise what was going on, it had encircled her body and her legs above the knees.

He pulled her backwards onto the ground and she could only lie there helpless, seeing the same thing happen to the Marquis.

He was swearing, but, as soon as he had pushed him down, the big man brought a cotton handkerchief from his pocket and gagged him.

"Stop! You must not do – that!" Odela tried to cry.

Even as she spoke the words, Fred Cotter gagged her, tying the knot tightly at the back of her head.

"Now," he gloated, "you're both goin' a short distance to a secret place where nobody'll ever find you."

As he spoke, he picked Odela up in his arms and walking past the stone fountain moved towards the door.

She wondered where they were being taken.

Then when they went out into the sunshine she thought that it must be to the woods.

To her surprise Fred Cotter moved along the side of the Folly and then stopped.

He put her down on the ground and pulled up what appeared to be an iron grating from the foot of the Folly.

A second later he disappeared through it.

The huge man who was carrying the Marquis put him down and picked up Odela and pushed her through the grating feet first and Fred Cotter, who was waiting inside took her in his arms.

For a moment after the sunshine outside Odela could see nothing.

Then she realised that she was in a cellar underneath the Folly and there was a faint light coming from somewhere so that she could just see the outline of where she was.

Fred Cotter put her down on the ground.

He then went to the grating to pull the Marquis through it and put him down beside Odela.

Then he stood looking at them both with an evil expression on his face.

"Here you'll stay," he sneered, "until I come to see if the worms have eaten you. And that'll teach you not to interfere with me again!"

He laughed.

Because it echoed round the walls it was an ugly eerie sound, which made Odela shiver.

Then he walked back to the grating and climbed out with the help of the big man outside.

Odela heard the cover being put back into place and then there was the sound of rattling stones.

She knew that Fred Cotter and his accomplice were covering the lower part of the grating with earth and stones, so that it would not be noticed by anybody who might come to the Folly.

With a sinking feeling of horror she realised that this was very unlikely.

The Marquis had already told her that he had forbidden anyone to come near it and that was exactly what the crooked Fred Cotter wanted.

She wondered what he would do about their horses and then she thought that perhaps, by good luck, he would not realise that they were there.

Surely somebody would see them eventually and investigate the whereabouts of their owners?

Her eyes were now growing more accustomed to the darkness of the cellar and she could see more clearly.

To her surprise, they were not the only occupants of their prison.

A packing case attracted her attention first, quite a small one but closed and behind it she saw the frame of a picture, in fact there were two of them.

Then she looked to the other side and thought that she could make out a large Chinese vase.

There were several other items besides a number of roughly wrapped parcels.

It was then she realised why Fred Cotter had never been convicted on the charges brought against him for robbery.

This was where he had hidden all his spoils and he would take them out only when he had arranged for a dealer to purchase them.

It was indeed a clever plot.

With a sinking heart Odela realised that no one had ever thought for a moment that this was where they might be hidden.

The Marquis moved and she realised that he was pushing himself back so that he could sit upright against the wall behind them.

Because the ground was hard and uncomfortable, Odela thought that she would do the same as, because the rope was so tight, it was becoming even more painful.

Then, as she pushed her head back, she had an idea.

Fred Cotter had gagged her.

But the gag was tied over her chignon into which she had twisted her hair under her riding hat.

Her hair was so long that when she rode she invariably twisted it into a chignon, which she started high up at the back of her head so that a great deal of her hair was under her hat.

Now she thought that she might be able to rub out her hairpins and if she could do that, her hair would fall down her back and loosen the gag.

She then moved backwards and forwards against the wall and the Marquis, who was sitting up, was watching her.

Finally, as Odela shook her head, there was the faint tinkle as two hairpins fell to the ground.

A moment later by moving her lips as violently as she could, the gag slipped over her chin.

"I am – free," she exclaimed. "Now I can talk to you. How could this – have happened?"

The Marquis could not answer, but she knew how much he wanted to.

She studied him for a moment and then she said,

"If somehow you can move closer to me, I might be able to undo the back of your gag with my teeth,"

He could not answer, he only did as she suggested.

With some difficulty he managed to manoeuvre his head so that the back of it was as near to her lips as possible.

The cotton handkerchief was tightly knotted and it took Odela a long time.

She began to feel exhausted by the effort and she was also suffering with the weight of the Marquis's body against her shoulder.

Then suddenly and unexpectedly the handkerchief slipped.

"Thank God!" the Marquis cried.

He propelled himself back into his former position before he asked,

"How can you have been so clever? But now we have to escape!"

"But – how?" Odela asked.

"In the same way that you released my gag I will undo the ropes that bind you," he said. "Turn over onto your side."

"Do you – really think – you can – do it?"

"I shall need a lot of luck and your prayers," the Marquis answered.

"You know – you have those," Odela answered, "but how could we have imagined when we came here that – this was where Fred Cotter kept all the things he had stolen?"

"What I am asking myself is why I was fool enough to show him any mercy," the Marquis groaned. "It is something that will not happen again!"

"He means – us to – die here," Odela said in a frightened voice.

"Then he is going to be disappointed," the Marquis replied. "Turn sideways."

Odela did as she was told.

Although it took a long time, she could feel the Marquis working with his teeth on the ropes that bound her.

It was a thick coarse rope and Odela was sure that, because Fred Cotter and his accomplice had tied it round them so quickly and so skilfully, it was a routine that they had had a great deal of practice at.

'Perhaps he has left a number of other people to die here in the same wicked way,' she thought with horror.

It must have been nearly an hour later before the Marquis gave an exclamation of triumph.

Then the rope began to slacken from around her body.

For a moment Odela could hardly believe that it was true.

Then, as she moved and shook herself, she was free.

"You have – done it!" she cried. "You have done it. Now I must – undo you."

Sitting beside the Marquis Odela struggled with the rope, which had been tied with all the strength of the big man behind him.

It flashed through her mind that perhaps it would be easier to fetch somebody to help her and then she knew that it would be very humiliating for the Marquis to be found trussed up and helpless.

"I suppose you don't happen to be carrying a knife?" she asked hopefully him.

"I have already thought of that," the Marquis replied, "and I have cursed myself for not thinking one might be necessary."

"How could we have expected anything like this – to happen?" Odela asked.

Then she had an idea.

Looking across at the pile of things that Fred Cotter had stolen, she said,

"Let's see if there is something here that I can cut your ropes with."

She did not wish to depress the Marquis, but she realised that it was going to be a Herculean task to undo the thick rope with her long thin fingers.

Without waiting for him to agree she jumped up and pulled the coverings from the parcels one by one.

There were snuffboxes with exquisitely enamelled lids, which she was sure were unique and very valuable.

There were a number of bronzes that were skilfully made and there was a collection of miniatures that had obviously come from some ancestral home like Coombe Court.

Then just as she was despairing of finding anything there was a long leather box.

She opened it and gave a cry of relief.

"What have you found?" the Marquis asked hopefully.

"A pair of very elaborate carvers!" she replied.

She picked up the knives.

As she did so, she saw that the box was embellished with the Coat of Arms of what she thought must be a London Livery Company.

She was, however, concerned only with the long fine steel blade.

It had a very elaborate silver-gilt handle as did the fork that rested in its groove beside it.

She ran to the Marquis and knelt down beside him.

The knife was sharp and it took her only a few minutes to cut through the ropes.

The Marquis shook himself free of them and Odela was still kneeling as he pulled the last rope from around his knees.

Then he bent forward and putting his arms around her said,

"Thank you, my darling! I don't believe that any other woman in the world could have been so wonderful!"

Before she could move and before she could realise what was happening, his lips were on hers.

He kissed her fiercely and demandingly, as if he was afraid that this was something he had thought he would never be able to do.

For a second Odela could only feel surprise.

Then, as his lips made hers captive, a strange sensation invaded her whole body.

It moved like lightning from her breasts into her lips.

She knew then that this was what she had wanted and this was why she had felt happy when she was coming to the Folly.

The few minutes that they had been together before Fred Cotter arrived had been an enchantment beyond words.

The Marquis raised his head to look down at her.

Then without saying a word he was kissing her again, kissing her possessively and passionately.

Without thinking she put up her hand as if to protect herself and instantly she was free, but it was impossible to speak.

She could only gaze up at the Marquis with eyes that seemed to fill her small face.

Even in the dim light of the cellar he could see that they were shining like stars.

The Marquis rose to his feet.

"Let's get out of this *damned* place," he urged her. "I have never been in such a tight corner before and it is thanks entirely to you that we are alive."

Because the ceiling was so low he had to bend his head to walk towards the grating.

He pushed it open and turned to hold out his hand to Odela.

She followed him and, as she reached him, the light was on her face.

"I have so much to say to you, my precious," he said, "but first we have to catch and imprison that devil before he does any more harm."

"Yes – of course," Odela agreed.

At the same time she felt that nothing mattered except that she was with the Marquis.

Now she admitted to herself that she loved him.

"I will fetch our hats," the Marquis said.

Odela waited outside as he went back into the Folly.

As she stood in the sunshine, it was hard to believe that they might have died in the cellar.

'Thank You God – thank You,' she whispered and felt strongly that her mother was very near her.

The Marquis returned and they then walked to the other side of the Folly.

As Odela had hoped, Fred Cotter had not found their horses and Dragonfly and Saracen were still waiting patiently behind the Folly.

It was only as they reached them that Odela was aware that her hair was falling over her shoulders.

She caught hold of it and began to twist it.

"That is how I want you to look," the Marquis said, "and how you should have looked when you were the Sleeping Princess from *Sleeping Beauty*!"

Odela gave a shaky little laugh.

She managed to twist her hair into some sort of shape and then she pinned it with the two hairpins that had not fallen out.

She put on her riding hat with its gauze veil and the Marquis lifted her onto Dragonfly's saddle.

Pulling her riding skirt into place he looked up at her and said quietly,

"I suppose you know how wonderful you have been, but I will tell you all about it when we have more time."

He mounted Saracen before she could make any reply.

She knew, because of the look in his eyes and the way he had spoken, that her heart had turned several somersaults.

Only when they had ridden side by side down into the wood did Odela say,

"We ought – not ride back to – Coombe Court together."

"I have been thinking about that," the Marquis replied, "and, if you will go home, I will call the Chief Constable and have Cotter and that criminal with him arrested as soon as possible."

Odela gave a little exclamation and he added quickly,

"I will try to keep your name out of this drama altogether and unless Cotter gives you away, which I think is unlikely, no one need know that you were with me."

"Oh, please – try to do – so," Odela began.

"You do realise that I have to know the truth sooner or later and that I must see you?"

"Y-yes – of course."

The Marquis thought for a moment.

And then he asked,

"What time does Nanny go to bed?"

"Early," Odela replied, "usually at about half-past-nine."

"Then you come to the library at ten o'clock."

"I – will – try."

"I shall be waiting for you."

He put out his hand and, when she put hers into it, he kissed her fingers.

"Take care of yourself, my beautiful Sleeping Princess and I will make certain that there will be no more rampaging dragons to frighten you."

He smiled at her as she spoke and raised his hat.

Then he was riding away into the wood as Odela rode off in the opposite direction.

As she went, she was saying more prayers of thankfulness and gratitude.

They had been saved by the mercy of God from what might have been a slow death from starvation.

Then their bodies would have rotted until only the bones were left.

The only alternative to such a Fate would have been if somebody had found the horses and even then it would have taken a very astute person to guess that there was a cellar beneath the Folly.

It would never have occurred to anybody living locally that Fred Cotter would have hidden his loot there,

'We have been lucky, very very lucky!' she mused.

She realised too how humiliating it would have been for the Marquis if they had been found roped and imprisoned.

And as far as she was concerned it would have been disastrous.

It was then for the first time she questioned if the Marquis loved her as much as she loved him.

When he had kissed her, she had felt as if they were joined not only physically but spiritually by God Himself.

The Marquis was the man of her dreams, the man she had always believed she would meet some day.

There could be no one else in her life except her 'Dream Lover'.

But for him there had been many women, including the beautiful Lady Beaton whom he had just taken back to London.

She could clearly remember what the Head Housemaid had said about him and the way that quite a number of the servants who came to call on Nanny had said how handsome he was.

They also implied that there were a great number of women only too ready to tell him so.

'Perhaps he is only interested in me because I am new and mysterious,' Odela pondered.

Quite suddenly she was afraid – afraid of being disillusioned.

Afraid too of being hurt.

But how could she be anything else when she could feel the love that she had for the Marquis pulsating through her whole body?

When he had kissed her, it had been the most wonderful thing that could ever have happened to her.

It had been a rapture and an ecstasy beyond anything she could imagine.

She had felt, even in that strange dark place where they had been left to die an inglorious death, as if she had reached Heaven itself.

'I love him so much!' she thought desperately, 'and the most sensible thing I could do now would be to go and hide myself somewhere else.'

Then she knew that it was something she dare not do.

She had not been frightened before because she had known that she was going to Nanny.

But if she went off alone there might perhaps be more men like Fred Cotter to injure and terrify her.

There might also be men who would also want to kiss her, as the Marquis had done, because she was pretty.

She suddenly thought that, if he was only interested in her because she had a pretty face, she would want to die.

Yet she knew that it was such a strong feeling and it came from the very depths of her heart.

She would never love another man in the same way that she loved the Marquis.

CHAPTER SEVEN

The Marquis went into the library at a quarter-to-ten.

The fire was burning brightly and he lit more candles than had been left by the footmen and sat down to look up at his ancestor's portrait.

He was somewhat afraid that Odela would be too nervous to come to him.

Then after he had waited for about fifteen minutes the door opened and she came in.

To his surprise her hair was hanging over her shoulders and she was wearing what he realised was a very pretty but simple dressing gown.

She ran towards him and said in a breathless voice,

"I only – came to – tell you that I – cannot come to – you as we had – planned."

"But you are here," he replied.

"Only to – tell you that I – cannot come – because I have had to – undress."

She thought that he looked surprised and went on,

"Betty was – restless and Nanny could not go to bed. She came in and – helped me to – take off my – gown.

She smiled at him before saying,

"There was – nothing I could – do. She would have thought it – very strange if I – had dressed again."

"I understand," the Marquis commented, "but equally you look very lovely as you are and I am sure that, if Nanny thinks you are in bed, she will not now disturb you."

"I cannot be – certain of – that."

"I would like you to take a chance on it," the Marquis suggested with a smile. "I am sure that you will want to know what happened to Fred Cotter."

"Yes – of course – I do," she agreed, "but I-I feel – shy because I look – like this."

"Forget it," the Marquis urged, "and let me tell you what happened after we left each other in the wood."

Because she was intensely curious Odela did as he advised and sat down in a high-backed armchair.

The Marquis sat opposite her and they were on each side of the fireplace.

Odela clasped her hands together arid bent forward. She did not want to miss a word of what the Marquis was saying.

"I went, as I told you I was going to do," he began, "straight to the Chief Constable. He lives only about two miles away. As luck would have it, as I arrived, he was having a consultation with senior members of the Police Force in the neighbourhood."

Odela gave a little exclamation, but she did not interrupt.

"We went almost at once to Fred Cotter's house and caught him and his accomplice red-handed."

"Red-handed?" Odela questioned.

"They were packing up a piece of jewellery that Cotter had stolen some time ago and for which he had presumably just found a buyer."

"I thought that was the way he – worked," Odela said in a low voice.

"You are quite right," the Marquis affirmed, "and Cotter is now safely behind bars in Oxford."

"Oh, I am glad – so very glad!" Odela cried.

"His accomplice has also been taken into custody," the Marquis continued, "and I learnt, which somewhat excused my helplessness in his hands, that he was a pugilist at one time."

"He – might have – hurt you!" Odela exclaimed.

"He might indeed," the Marquis agreed, "but actually he is a strange character because he is dumb."

Odela remembered that the big man had not said a word all the time they were being tied up.

"Apparently," the Marquis explained, "when he was fighting somebody of his own weight he bit his tongue almost in half. After the doctors had operated on it he was unable to speak."

"It must have been – awful for – him," Odela said. "At the same time – because he is – so large he is a very – frightening man."

"As he will be going to prison with Cotter, I don't think we need think about him anymore."

"And they will not be – able to – threaten you again?" Odela said.

"Neither will they frighten you," the Marquis assured her. "The Chief Constable agreed that your name need not be mentioned and actually, as I do not wish to lie in the witness box, I simply said that you were a friend and he therefore thought that you were a guest of mine from London."

"Oh – thank you – *thank you*!" Odela cried. "I was so – frightened that – "

She stopped.

"Frightened of who?" the Marquis enquired.

"I-I do *not* – want to – talk about – it."

The Marquis bent forward in his chair.

"We have just been through a traumatic experience together, Odela. How can you continue not to trust me?"

He paused a moment and then went on,

"You know I would do anything to help you, not only because I am sorry for you but for another reason as well."

"What is – that?" Odela asked.

As she spoke, her eyes met the Marquis's.

She felt that he must be aware of how much she loved him as she waited for his reply.

Then before he could speak the door of the library opened.

As it did so, the Marquis, with the quickness of a man of action, rose to his feet.

He realised that Odela was sitting in a high-backed armchair with its back to the door and she therefore would not be seen by anyone who had just come into the library.

It was Newton and the Marquis walked towards him.

"What do you want, Newton?" he asked. "I am busy."

"I'm sorry, my Lord, to disturb you," Newton replied, "but a lady and gentleman have just called to see your Lordship."

"At this late hour?" the Marquis exclaimed. "Who are they?"

"It's the Countess of Shalford, my Lord, and the Viscount More."

The Marquis said nothing and Newton went on,

"They says it's of the utmost importance that they see your Lordship immediately."

"Offer them some refreshment and say I will join them in a few minutes," the Marquis ordered.

"Very good, my Lord."

Newton withdrew.

As the Marquis turned round, Odela rose from the chair where she was sitting and ran towards him.

She flung herself against him saying in a terrified whisper,

"Hide me – please hide me – they have – come for me – but I cannot go – with them! Oh, please – hide me!"

Her voice was pathetic and there were tears in her eyes.

The Marquis put his arms around her.

. "Why do they want you?" he asked.

"The Countess is my – stepmother and she – insists that – I marry – the Viscount and – he – "

Odela paused and even through her tears she blushed before she hid her face and mumbled,

"is – her – lover!"

The Marquis's arms tightened.

"But – why?" he asked. "Why should your stepmother want you to do such a thing?"

"Because – Mama left – me a lot – of money – and the Viscount is – poor."

"I know your father. He is a very distinguished man," the Marquis said. "Surely he would not allow such a thing?"

"He always – does what – Stepmama wants and – when she is determined – no one can stand up – against her."

Odela's voice was now stifled with tears as she said again.

"Please – please – hide me and – quickly. I would – rather die than – marry any man – except – "

She stopped.

She realised that what she had been about to say was very revealing.

She hid her head against the Marquis's shoulder and she could feel her whole body trembling.

He could feel her body quivering against him through the thin fabric of her nightclothes.

"Now, listen," he said quietly, "I want you to stay here where you will be safe and to make sure of it I will lock the door and take the key with me."

He smiled at her and then continued,

"I will get rid of them and when I come back we will plan how your stepmother cannot do anything so outrageous as to marry you to a man you do not love."

"You – promise – you will not – tell them where – I am?" Odela asked raising her head.

"Do you still not trust me?" the Marquis asked.

He looked down at her and tears were running down her cheeks and her long eyelashes were wet.

Yet he thought that she was lovelier than anyone he had ever seen before in his whole life.

He bent his head and very gently kissed her lips.

"Wait here," he said. "I promise you that everything will be all right."

He took his arm from her and walked towards the door.

When he closed it behind him, Odela heard the key turn in the lock and she then put up her hands to her face feeling that this could not be happening to her.

She wondered how it was possible for her stepmother to have found her.

Then she guessed that it must have been through Fred Cotter.

He knew who she was and, because he had been arrested, the news of it would be all over the County.

And doubtless they were talking about it at Shalford House.

She could not believe that her stepmother was actually here in Coombe Court.

She moved back to the fireplace and sat down not in the armchair but on the sofa that faced the fire.

From there she could see the door.

She thought if anyone tried to come into the library she would hide from them, perhaps behind the curtains.

Because she felt so frightened she started to pray.

Her prayers were even more fervent than when she and the Marquis were tied up in the cellar of the Folly.

At least then they had been together.

If her stepmother took her away now, she would be powerless in her hands and before she could realise what was happening to her she would find herself married to the Viscount.

'Help me – Mama – *help me*!' she prayed, 'and let me – stay with – the Marquis.'

She thought if she could do so, she would do anything, even to being a servant in his household.

At least if she was under his roof she would feel safe.

"I love – him!" she murmured aloud.

She knew that he would try to save her, but would he be strong enough to defy her stepmother who always got her own way?

It seemed to Odela that a century went by and she was beginning to think that her stepmother must have succeeded in convincing the Marquis that she should go back with them to Shalford Hall.

Then she heard footsteps and sprang to her feet.

Before the key had turned in the lock and the door was opened she had run to the end of the library.

She hid herself behind the crimson velvet curtain that she had watched Fred Cotter through.

The Marquis came into the room and he closed the door behind him and walked to the fireplace.

"Odela," he called out softly.

There was a little pause and then Odela peeped out from behind the curtain as if to make sure that he was alone.

When she saw that he was indeed alone, she gave a cry and ran towards him.

Before she reached him the Marquis held out his arms.

He pulled her close against him.

Then he was kissing her, kissing her passionately, fiercely and demandingly.

She thought that he lifted her from a hell of uncertainty and fear into Heaven.

Now there were only the stars and a rapture beyond any words.

He kissed her until the library and the house itself seemed to swing dizzily round them.

As he drew her closer and closer still, Odela could feel his heart beating frantically, just as hers was.

Only when the wonder of it was too marvellous to be borne did she give a little murmur and hide her face against his neck.

He carried her to the sofa and sat down.

He cradled her in his arms as if she was a baby and then he kissed her again until they were both breathless.

"Why did you not tell me?" he asked at last. "How can you have let that woman menace you in such a disgraceful manner?"

"Y-you have – sent – her away?" Odela stammered.

"I have sent her away saying that I will bring you to your home tomorrow before luncheon."

Odela felt as if she was turned to stone.

"You have – told her – that? H-how could you – do such – a thing?"

The Marquis smiled.

"We will call on her, but she cannot make you stay."

"But she – will! She – will!" Odela cried, "and she will – force Papa to – give his consent to my – marriage to the – Viscount!"

"Unfortunately for him she will not be able to do that," the Marquis said.

"What – do you – mean? He will – if my stepmother – insists."

"You are being very stupid, my precious," the Marquis smiled, "and once again you are not trusting me. I am cleverer than your stepmother!"

"But – how? What – are you – saying? I-I don't understand."

"I got rid of them," the Marquis explained, "by saying that it was too late to disturb you as you slept in the nursery with my niece who is not well."

Odela thought that this was clever of him, but she did not say so and he went on,

"They had heard that you were here because Fred Cotter had cursed you all the time he was being taken through the village by the Police."

Odela made a little murmur of horror, but the Marquis continued,

"I assured your stepmother that you were perfectly well and safe and I would bring you to Shalford Hall tomorrow where, of course, she and the Viscount, who professes to be madly in love with you, will be waiting."

"Then – you believed – what she – told you!" Odela said in a defeated little voice.

"She lied like a trooper!" the Marquis replied, "and I did not believe one word of anything she said."

"Then – why are you – taking me – back?"

"Because by the time I do so and, of course, I shall be delighted to meet your father again, my precious little Princess – you and I will be married!"

Odela stared at him as if she thought that she could not have heard him aright.

"*M-married?*" she whispered.

"Married!" the Marquis affirmed. "I have already sent my secretary to tell the Vicar, who is also my Chaplain, that we will be married tomorrow at ten o'clock in the morning here in my own Chapel."

He smiled.

"After that, my lovely one, we will set off on our honeymoon, stopping only on the way so that you may introduce me to your father."

"I don't – believe this!" Odela cried. "Can I – really be your – wife? Do you – love – me?"

The questions seemed to tumble over themselves.

The Marquis pulled her close to him again.

"Do you doubt it?" he asked, "and I promise you, Odela, it is something I shall prove once you are mine."

He would have kissed her, but Odela hid her face against him again.

"Are you – sure," she asked in a muffled tone, "really – sure that you –want me? I love you! I love you – with all – my heart and soul, but I do – *not* want you to – marry me – out of pity."

The Marquis laughed and it was a very happy sound.

"Do you really think that I would do anything so foolish?" he asked. "If I was just sorry for you, my adorable one, I could spirit you away to any part of the world you wished to go."

His voice deepened.

"But I want you. I want you as I have never wanted a woman before and I think, after all we have been through together, we shall be very very happy living here with our horses and, of course, our children."

He felt Odela quiver in his arms, and then she turned her face up to his.

He kissed her very gently at first, as if he dedicated his life to her.

Then his kisses became more demanding and more passionate, but she was not afraid.

She knew that this was the love she had so often prayed for.

The love that was not only soft and gentle but strong, demanding and irresistible.

"I love you! *I love – you!*" she wanted to call out, but there was really no need for words.

*

Odela awoke and knew that she had been dreaming of the Marquis.

It was eight o'clock and the sun outside was shining brightly.

She could hear the clink of cups and plates, which told her that breakfast was being laid in the nursery.

For a moment she thought that she must have dreamt what had happened last night.

But she could still feel the Marquis's lips on hers.

At the thought of him her heart throbbed in a very strange manner and a little thrill ran through her body.

She climbed slowly out of bed and, while she was washing, Nanny came in to ask,

"Now, what's goin' on, that's what I wants to know! I've just been informed by Mr. Newton that his Lordship wants you downstairs at fifteen minutes to ten and he's sent you these."

As Nanny spoke, she put two parcels down on the bed.

Odela guessed what they contained and she finished drying her face before she replied,

"Last night, Nanny, Stepmama came here with the Viscount to take me home."

Nanny gave an exclamation of horror but, before she could speak, Odela went on,

"The Marquis saved me and they went away again."

"How did they know you were here?" Nanny asked.

Odela thought that there was no time to tell her about Fred Cotter, so she merely shook her head.

"You said his Lordship saved you," Nanny queried. "How did he do that?"

Odela smiled.

"You are not – to be angry with me, Nanny. But I have met him several times since I have been here and now – we are going to be married!"

Nanny stared at her for a moment.

Then she gave a cry of delight.

"*Married*!" she exclaimed. "Well, that's just what I've been wishin' for you and this house has the best nurseries I've ever been in!"

Odela laughed.

At the same time she felt near to tears because it was all so wonderful and beautiful.

Then, as Nanny realised just what was happening, she helped her into a pretty white gown that had been in the saddlebags.

The parcels from the Marquis contained a lace veil that reached from her head to her feet and it also made a small train behind her.

Then there was a diamond tiara set as sprays of flowers.

"You couldn't look lovelier if you was goin' to Buckingham Palace!" Nanny remarked when she was dressed.

"It's far more important that I should be – with the Marquis than with the Queen," Odela replied. "Oh, Nanny, do you think I look pretty enough – for him?"

She was thinking of Lady Beaton and the other beautiful women that the housemaids had talked about.

"You're as lovely as your mother was," Nanny professed. "She was the most beautiful person I've ever seen and I can't say fairer than that."

"That is all I want to hear," Odela smiled.

She kissed Nanny before she went downstairs.

"God bless you, my baby," Nanny said with tears in her eyes, "and may you always be as happy as you look at this moment."

"I will be," Odela replied confidently.

She felt as if she had wings on her heels as she went down the stairs from the nurseries.

When she reached the first floor, she walked along the passage until she came to the main staircase.

She knew instinctively that the Marquis would be waiting for her in the hall.

He watched her coming down the stairs towards him and he was so sure that she was everything he had ever wanted, but thought he would never find.

He had known when he first kissed her that she had never been kissed before.

He was the first man in her life and would be the last.

In all his experience with women he had never loved any of them in the same way that he loved Odela.

It was not only her beauty that entranced him or the spiritual purity that came from her.

It was because, just as his instinct told him that she was his, he was aware that hers reacted in the same way.

They were already one person even before they were united by the Sacrament of Marriage.

*

The Chapel at Coombe Court, which had been built at the same time as the house, was consecrated when it had been opened

As the marriage would be performed by the private Chaplain to the Marquis of Trancombe there was no need for any legal formality.

The Marquis gave Odela his arm and they walked down the long passage that led to the Chapel.

As they went, he thought that this was exactly the sort of marriage he wanted.

He had been sure, however, that it was something he would never have.

He knew that for both of them the Marriage Service would be a Ceremony that they would always remember.

There would be no so-called 'friends' to criticize, to be envious or to spoil what to Odela would be a Sacred Ceremony.

He realised that she was feeling a little nervous.

He put his hand over hers where it lay on his arm and he felt a little quiver go through her.

'I will protect her and keep her happy for the rest of her life,' he vowed, 'and no one shall ever frighten her again.'

He knew that no other woman of his acquaintance would have been as brave as Odela had been when they had been at the mercy of Fred Cotter.

No other woman would have been brave enough to run away from her stepmother.

Or be clever enough to go to her old Nanny for protection.

'She is unique,' he told himself.

When they knelt to receive the Blessing, the Marquis prayed that he would be worthy of her.

'She must never be disappointed in me,' he pledged.

*

The Marquis and Marchioness of Trancombe drove away from Shalford Hall and their Chaise was drawn by four perfectly matched horses.

The Marquis managed his horses, Odela knew, with an expertise that was brilliant.

But for the moment all she could see was the astonishment and frustration on her stepmother's face!

She also did not miss the satisfaction on her father's.

She put out her hand and laid it on the Marquis's knee.

"Have we really escaped?" she asked him in a whisper.

"We have," the Marquis said triumphantly.

He too had realised that the announcement that they were married had been a blow to the Countess that she had not expected.

She had gone pale with anger.

They had all three been waiting for the Marquis and Odela to arrive.

It was the Earl who had come forward to say,

"Thank you, my Lord, for bringing my daughter back. I have been very worried about her."

He had shaken the Marquis by the hand and Odela had kissed her father saying,

"I was quite safe, Papa, with Nanny."

"I know that now, my dearest," her father replied, "but your stepmother was extremely upset when you disappeared."

"That is something I will never do again," Odela promised the Marquis.

"That is true," he said before anybody else could speak, "and I feel sure that you will congratulate me when you know that Odela is now my wife and we are both very happy!"

There had been a sudden silence.

Then before the Earl could say that he was delighted, which he actually was, the Countess had exclaimed, her voice a scream,

"It's not true! I don't believe it!"

"It is quite true," the Marquis replied, "and, as I realised last night that I could not lose Odela not for a day, not even for an hour, we were married this morning."

"It's illegal!" the Countess snapped.

"I think you will find difficulty in proving that allegation," the Marquis said quietly.

It was then that the Earl recovered his breath.

"If my daughter is happy that is all that matters," he smiled, "and, of course, I am delighted to have a son-in-law who lives next door."

"I am very very happy, Papa," Odela smiled.

The Marquis did not allow anybody else to say very much more.

He explained that they were in a hurry to go to one of his houses, which was some distance away and he knew that they would understand if they left immediately.

The Viscount had said nothing and Odela did not address a word to him.

She could not help feeling that he was somewhat relieved that he did not have to be married.

Even though he might miss her money.

*

It was only now when she was alone with the Marquis that Odela remembered that she had not told him how rich she was.

Then she told herself that it was unimportant.

She was quite certain that he would find many ways for her to spend her money on things that really mattered.

Schools, hospitals and help for those who were genuinely in need.

'He is so rich himself that it will not make any difference to him one way or the other,' she thought, 'so why should we waste time in talking about it?'

She moved a little closer to him.

"I love you!" she sighed.

The Marquis smiled.

"And I adore you, my beautiful one, and tonight when we are in the house where we are starting our honeymoon, I will tell you exactly how much."

"Tell – me now," Odela pleaded with him.

"I love you! I adore you! I worship you!"

Her eyes were radiant as he spoke.

She felt that the horses' hoofs, as they travelled on, were saying the words over and over again.

That was all she wanted and she knew that it would be the foundation of their lives from now on.

The Marquis glanced at her grey eyes looking at him adoringly.

"We have rid ourselves of the second dragon," he said, "and now, my Sleeping Princess, all I have to do is to awaken you not with a kiss but with love."

"That is – what I – want," Odela answered. "Oh, my darling, darling husband, you are so – wonderful and I find it very – hard to – believe that I am really your – wife."

"If you say things like that," the Marquis answered, "I shall kiss you and then we shall have an accident."

Odela gave a little laugh. ,

"No one could drive as well as you."

"That is what I want you to think," he said, "just as I want you to believe that I am wonderful and to keep telling me so. But not when my hands are otherwise engaged!"

Odela laughed again.

Then in a whisper that he could hardly hear she murmured,

"I love – you – *I love – you*!"

He felt as if they were driving into the heat of the sun.

They were no longer human but one with the Gods.

This was life, this was love.

This was the adventure that Odela had always dreamt of having in her life and she was no longer afraid.

OTHER BOOKS IN THIS SERIES

The Barbara Cartland Eternal Collection is the unique opportunity to collect all five hundred of the timeless beautiful romantic novels written by the world's most celebrated and enduring romantic author.

Named the Eternal Collection because Barbara's inspiring stories of pure love, just the same as love itself, the books will be published on the internet at the rate of four titles per month until all five hundred are available.

The Eternal Collection, classic pure romance available worldwide for all time.